I VISIT
THE SOVIETS

I VISIT THE SOVIETS

The Provincial Lady in Russia

by E.M. Delafield

Drawings by Leo Manso

Cassandra
Editions

Academy Chicago Publishers, 425 N. Michigan Ave., Chicago 60611

Published in 1985 by
Academy Chicago Publishers
425 N. Michigan Ave.
Chicago, Illinois 60611

Library of Congress Cataloging-in-Publication Data

Delafield, E.M., 1890–1943.
    The provincial lady in Russia.

    Reprint. Originally published: I visit the Soviets.
New York : Harper & Brothers, 1937.
    Includes index.
    I. Title.
PR6007.E33I2   1985   823'.912   85-18611
ISBN 0-89733-156-7

CONTENTS

ILLUSTRATIONS

COMMUNE

(1)

IT WAS IN THE INCONGRUOUS SET-ting of an expensive London restaurant that an American publisher was moved to exclaim to an astonished dinner-guest whose novels he had published for years:

"I wish to Heavens you'd go and live on a Collective Farm in Russia for six months, and write a funny book about it."

"Funny?"

"Sure. Nobody has been at all funny yet, about Russia."

I admitted that I thought I probably might be funny enough *in* Russia, but that I didn't think I could be very funny *about* it. Especially not about a Collective Farm.

"Besides, they wouldn't have me there."

"That could be arranged," he replied firmly—and, as I afterwards discovered, without the faintest justification.

"They'd expect me to work, and I don't know anything about farming."

"I dare say you could help about the house," said my publisher blithely. "Anyhow, you could make plenty of contacts, and get a slant on the women's point of view. It's a grand idea!"

Not only did I not think it a grand idea, but I had no faintest intention of putting it into action.

"Have some caviar," my publisher said—perhaps with some thought of making me more Soviet-minded—and I hope it was from kindness and hospitality only that he also offered me some excellent champagne.

"Then in the evenings," he went on dreamily, "they all sit round and talk — you know what Russians are—and tell you the stories of their lives."

"That would be perfectly splendid, except that I don't know a word of Russian."

"I dare say you can learn it before you go. It's not as difficult as people think. And anyway, some of them would speak a little English or German or something. You'd be able to make out quite a lot. And I guess that what you didn't understand, you could make up."

I guessed I could, too—but I had no desire to put it to the test.

I explained that it was all quite out of the question—I couldn't leave my home, my children, my work—and in any case they certainly wouldn't have me on any farm.

Then I tried not to feel that I was drinking the champagne and eating the caviar on false pretences.

About twenty-four hours later a dreadful and familiar feeling began to creep over me, that I might have to do this thing that I so little wished to do. My only real reason for *not* doing it, after all, was that I knew I should hate it. If one has been brought up in a convent-school, as I was, that particular reason is always and for evermore to be viewed with instinctive mistrust. There is nothing good or rational about this attitude of mind, and I have no wish to defend it. But it gets under one's skin at a very early age, and usually remains there for life.

Exactly like Mr. Bultitude, when he wished to

explain to Dr. Grimstone that his presence at home was indispensable, I said to myself: Everything will go to rack and ruin without me.

But would it?

On reflection, I saw that it wouldn't. My home was in a far less parlous state than that of poor Mr. Bultitude.

There was no reason at all why, with a little re-arrangement, anything should go to rack and ruin without me.

It would be no compliment to my son—fifteen —and my daughter—twelve—and both of them at school, to suppose that they would not perfectly understand the circumstances and approve of my making the most of such an opportunity for new experiences. At the worst, it would only mean that I should miss half of their summer holidays. (And I may say at once that they were thoroughly sympathetic and approving, as soon as they under-stood that it was all part of my work, and that I should run no risk either of starvation or of being flung into a Russian prison.) I wanted, also, to make quite sure that I *could* do without the civi-lized things and people to which I had become ac-customed, and that I was not dependent on any of

[4]

them.

Finally, the usual economic considerations influenced me, just as they influence everybody, except perhaps saints and geniuses.

Publishers, I suppose, acquire some strange and unnatural insight into the psychology of authors.

When I walked into the London office of my American publisher, three or four days after the caviar and champagne, he greeted me before I had spoken a word:

"When do you start for Russia?"

"The first week in May," I said grimly, "if you'll make it three months instead of six."

I knew he wouldn't.

We compromised on four.

I chose May because I knew that in South Russia, at any rate, it would be hot—and if I went then, I could get home in time for the last month of the summer holidays. Besides, it would give me time to learn some Russian.

From then until the day I sailed from London Docks for Leningrad, my prevalent attitude of mind was: "Who knows but the world may end tonight?"

The world, however, showed no signs of ending. The best, or worst, that happened was that I could get no assurance from anybody, either in London, or Moscow when I got there, that I should be allowed to stay on a farm except possibly as one of a "group" of tourists, shepherded by a guide-interpreter.

I was refused a "worker's visa" outright.

(Only Louis Fischer, the American journalist in Moscow, gave me any really practical advice and told me not to believe it couldn't be done.)

At intervals, a hope rose within me that I should have done my best and failed. This hope blazed brightest in Moscow, when I played my trump card—a personal letter of introduction to a Government official, and was told by him that what I suggested was impossible. The work on the farms was at its most intensive, and the arrival of an untrained hand would merely serve as an unwelcome interruption, he said firmly.

It sounded reasonable.

I could only think of one more card to play, and it was, again, the ghost of my convent upbringing that compelled me to play it.

I VISIT THE SOVIETS

I went to the American Embassy and asked for the only man there whom I knew by name. He was away on leave.

Then there really was no chance . . . but I heard myself enquiring who was doing his work.

"Another American."

"Please find out if he'll see me."

He saw me—which I think was good of him as I was neither an American citizen, nor could my name have conveyed anything whatever to him.

And when I outlined my farm plan and said that I had been told it would be impossible to arrange, he briskly remarked that there was one man who could certainly arrange it for me, and he would give me a letter to him right away. The man was an American, and lived in a city that I had had no intention of visiting—about twenty-four hours' journey from Moscow—Rostov-on-Don.

Two days later I went there—and a very hot and dirty journey it was. The train, like most Russian trains, started very late and, naturally, reached its destination very late. About 11 P. M. I went to the Intourist Hotel, and next day began the customary struggle to find the man I wanted. Every time I telephoned I was told either that "He is away" or "There is no reply"—two stock Russian phrases used, I believe, entirely in order to avoid having to take any further trouble.

At last I demanded to have a message sent to his house. The messenger—obtained with difficulty—took several hours to accomplish his mission, but came back at last and said: "He is away."

"Where has he gone?"

"I do not know. They did not say."

"When will he be back?"

"They do not know. Maybe tomorrow, maybe a few weeks."

"Was anybody in the house at all?"

"His wife."

"Doesn't *she* know when he'll be back?"

"She did not say."

"Give me her address and I will go and see her."

At this, everybody became deeply concerned. It was impossible: no trams went that way: I should lose myself: to send a special guide would be very expensive. I knew well that the last two objections, at all events, were only too well founded.

I VISIT THE SOVIETS

Perhaps, suggested the Intourist personnel, the lady would come and see me?

There seemed very little reason why she should do anything of the kind. Perhaps that was really why I agreed, and begged that she should be telephoned to once more, and asked if she would be good enough to visit me at the hotel.

She not only came—with un-Russian promptitude—but listened carefully to my request, had it all translated into Russian to make sure that she had understood it—and then told me about the Seattle Commune.

Her husband—(he really was away)—had been one of the pioneers in founding, in 1922, a communal farm, at the head of a group of American workers from Seattle, dissatisfied with conditions of living in the U.S.A. It was a state farm in the sense that a proportion of the profits went to the Soviet Government.

There was no reason in the world why I should not say that I was a friend of her husband's, said the Russian lady unscrupulously, and the Commune would be delighted to receive me, and would certainly find me something to do. Most of the workers were Russians, but there were always several there who had been in the States and were able to speak English.

I thanked her—I hope sounding more grateful than I really felt—and knew that the die was cast.

There were, of course, delays—the telephone at the farm was said several times to "make no reply" and there was even a suggestion that "they were all away": but in the end it was settled, as I knew it would be.

Seattle Commune had agreed to receive me on the following day.

(2)

It was a very hot day when I left Rostov and the train was, of course, very late. I was told, in the irresponsible Russian fashion, that it would arrive "at about eight" in the evening. Actually, it arrived at about a quarter to eleven. The station was a very tiny one, and nobody seemed to be there, although I had been told I should be met. I went into what seemed to be the stationmaster's office, and saw more cockroaches than I had ever seen before—but no other sign of life.

Then I went outside the station, and there a

youth spoke to me in Russian and asked if I was going to the Commune.

When I said that I was, he took me to a farm-lorry and I climbed into it with my bag, and we drove off—at first over a moderately good road and afterwards across a long tract of prairie-land.

The Commune was, as I learnt later, a settlement that had grown in twelve years from a single frame-and-thatch building to something rather like a small hamlet in the middle of a huge farm.

The total extent of it was 13,000 hectares.

On the first evening—or night, for it must have been the middle of the night by the time we arrived—I only saw an occasional electric light, and the dim outline of the single-storied dwelling-houses.

Into one of these my guide conducted me. It was a brick-built building with a cement floor. We turned into a doorway immediately on the right of the entrance, and went through a long bare room that held a wooden table, two benches and a picture of Stalin, and nothing else.

At the end of this room were two doors, numbered respectively 1 and 3. Into 1 I went, and it was the room in which I was to sleep.

It was a small room, about twelve feet by fourteen, I should think—and it contained four iron bedsteads, each with a straw pallet, a cushion stuffed with straw, two sheets and a cotton blanket. There were two windows in the room, a table and four wooden stools. Nothing else, except for an unshaded electric light bulb hanging from the ceiling. Neither blinds, curtains, strips of carpeting nor any toilet appliance whatsoever.

The young man indicated to me that I could take my choice of the beds, and that I should have the room to myself, at any rate for the remainder of that night.

Foreseeing that in another minute I should be alone, I asked him to tell me where I could wash. I had been seven hours travelling "hard" class, in a very dusty train—and had other requirements, even more urgent than soap and water.

But I could not make the young man understand my English—let alone my Russian. Finally, he said in a desperate way, "Come!" and we rushed out into the night again.

Only a few yards off was another lighted building—actually, it was the canteen—and from it my guide extracted a tall Armenian who spoke English.

My faith in my own powers of explaining what I wanted intelligibly, and at the same time discreetly, was now gone, and when he said—with an accent that made me think of a New York taxi-driver — "How-d'you-do? what you want?" — I replied with equal brevity, "How-d'you-do. I want the W.C."

"Uh-uh?"

"The water-closet."

"Oh, watter-closet! Sure. You see them two buildin's over there? The foist one men, the second one ladies. You'll find electric light, everythin' fine."

I thanked him and went.

The two buildings—little brick erections with what was only too evidently a cess-pit beneath each one — stood about fifty yards apart, and sure enough, an electric-light bulb shone, though rather dimly, in each.

I approached "ladies"—and next minute I knew exactly *how* communal, communal life can be.

There was no fastening on the door, and the elementary accommodation was provided for six persons at a time.

I VISIT THE SOVIETS

I had realized before coming to the Commune at all that any form of squeamishness on my part would be absurd and would defeat my own object, but I still think it was a severe test to have sprung upon one in the very first moment of arrival.

Before leaving the subject I may add that this was the only form of sanitation available and that the Comrades, so far as I ever found out, saw nothing objectionable about it.

I found my way back to my room, wondering whether I should find anybody else in the remaining beds—or, for that matter, in mine—but I was in sole possession.

I still had no idea where I could find water in which to wash, but I was dead tired, and the Armenian was nowhere to be seen, nor had I any wish to see him. He might have asked me what I thought of "ladies."

I did the best I could with a still-damp sponge, and the soap and towel I had in my bag, sprinkled Keatings liberally all over the sheets and pillow and pulled the bedstead as far away from the wall as I could.

Then I undressed and lay down on the straw pallet and slept.

(3)

Exactly as on one's first morning at school, the clanging of a bell—going on, as it seemed, for hours and hours—announced the day. I looked at my watch and saw that it was a quarter-past five. The only punctual thing I ever met in Russia was that bell.

Although it was so early it was broad daylight, and I could see people outside. (They could doubtless see me equally well through my uncurtained windows.)

Most of the men wore shirts, braces, and trousers that had obviously seen very long service.

The women nearly all had shawls or handkerchiefs over their heads, and coarse, shabby blouses and skirts. One or two wore flimsy, faded, printed-cotton frocks, probably purchased years before from a cheap store in America. Some were bare-footed, and a good many wore rubber-soled shoes. On that first morning it was very hot and sunny, and the ground was hard and dry.

I got up and—still inadequately washed—went across to the canteen at about half-past six. The clothes that I wore consisted of a navy-blue singlet, a very old linen skirt and canvas shoes, and I tied up my hair in a blue handkerchief. I also had thick boots and a leather jacket with me in case of wet weather—(and very inadequate they proved, when the time came).

Still feeling exactly like a new girl at school—with the additional disadvantage of knowing that I wasn't even a properly washed one—I entered the dining-hall.

It was a very large room, with a stage and curtains at one end of it, and two open hatches in the wall giving on to the kitchen. A number of wooden tables, with six or seven wooden stools round each, held a corresponding number of tin mugs and tin bowls. In the middle of the tables was a pile of black bread and a large enamel jug containing coffee. The bread was made on the farm and was good—the coffee was not real coffee, but made out of barley. It tasted of nothing in particular.

The Comrades ate in almost unbroken silence, and nobody took any notice of me, to my great relief, when I also sat down and began to eat black bread.

Presently, however, a peasant girl brought me

a mug of boiled milk and smiled very nicely when I thanked her.

Every day she brought me the boiled milk, and much as I abominated it, I always drank it gratefully.

Just as I had finished breakfast an elderly man came up and spoke to me in very fair English.

"Comrade Dashwood?"

(I always used my married name in Russia because both syllables are easy for Russian tongues and only "wood" is transformed into "vood.")

We shook hands, and he told me that he was the Secretary of the Commune, and offered to show me all over the farm, and to tell me anything that I wanted to know. He was a slow, amiable man, always pleasant and good-tempered, and—if possible—even more deliberate in his methods than were most of the Russians I met.

The following is a very brief résumé of the information about the Commune that I got from him, then and later.

Seattle was one of the only two Commune Settlements left out of many that had been started after the Revolution. Workers from America had come over and started it in 1922, and had found

[17]

exactly one house—or hut—in the midst of the vast expanse of steppe. Thirteen of them, including two women, had lived in this hut during the first months of incredible labour. They had lived mostly on tinned stores, sent from America.

Now, in 1936, there was a total population of 728, of whom 530 were workers. A number of lath-and-plaster dwelling-houses were erected, and there were five farm buildings made of bricks. The bricks were made on the estate. Indeed, everything came off the estate. They had their own electric-light plant, carpenter's shop, garage, repairing shed, bakery, and builder's yard.

Twenty-one tractors were in use, and there were 876 head of cattle. The horses—there were 56 of them—were never worked on the land. Many were kept for the Red Army, and some were used for drawing carts with straw, or manure, from one farm building to another. They were fine-looking animals, and seemed to me to have a much easier life than the people who looked after them.

I was shown with pride a stallion for which 6000 roubles had been paid, kept solely for breeding purposes. It rolled its eyes and snapped, and the Finn who showed it to me remarked that it was extremely savage, and to my great relief shut the door on it again. I thought he seemed rather re-lieved when I expressed no wish to look at it any longer.

In contrast to the stallion, the six bulls were of an almost incredible mildness. They were stalled in the same stables as the cows, and each was fastened by a chain that seemed to me to allow them a good deal of latitude in moving about.

However, they were all lying or sitting quietly there, more like sheep than bulls, and the Finn patted their large heads and invited me to do the same.

There was a poultry-yard—all white Leghorns—and bee-hives, and there were pigs. The majority of the pigs, however, were kept on a secondary part of the farm, about ten kilometres away from the main settlement.

Vines were also growing, and the vineyard was very large and flourishing. The orchards also were large but not flourishing. The worker in charge of them was despondent about the chances of getting any apples, any plums or any cherries. The trees were all limed and of a good size, and covered in leaves, but except for an occasional very small green cherry, there was no sign of fruit-bearing on any of them. Most of the trees had come from America, and it seemed that the soil was not suited to them.

It was heavy soil, black for a depth of about four inches, and after that all clay. I believe there were both oil and coal to be found in the region. Quantities of alfalfa grass grew everywhere.

The Secretary showed me nearly everything, and promised that I should visit the wheat-fields—where the wheat was already standing two feet high—and then he took me to his little wooden office, where there was a large typewriter, a table and two stools, a telephone, and the customary portraits of Lenin and Stalin on the walls.

On that first morning, actually, our conversation consisted of repeated requests on my part for some work to do, and of amiable evasions on his—but for the sake of convenience I set down here what I subsequently learned as to the general organization of life at the Commune.

The main principle of existence was that everything was held in common by the workers. When a certain proportion of the crops, and of all profits, had been sent to the Soviet Government, the remaining amount was divided between the workers. One rouble a day was deducted for each one's food. (I also paid that, all the time I was there.) Nobody handled any actual cash—except, I suppose, the Secretary, or Treasurer if they had one—but each person had a book in which to enter credits and debits.

A worker requiring money came and asked for it—but as most of them never left the Settlement at all, and nothing could be bought there—except a very few items, such as a village store in a remote part of Wales might have boasted twenty years ago—it was obvious that not much money was in circulation.

There was also a regulation, which was never thoroughly made clear to me, by which anybody coming to live at the Commune made a deposit of quite a large sum of money, which was forfeited if he ever left it again. If this was really the rule— and I believe it was—it seems a very arbitrary arrangement. It had not, however, prevented some from leaving. Quite a number had done so—and others, they told me, had been sent away—like novices in a religious order, told that they had no vocation to the life.

[21]

I asked what system of social legislation was in force, and learned that a Controlling Board of three members, elected by general ballot, existed to revise all plans for work, income and expenditure. At intervals they called a meeting of all the workers in each particular department, and invited suggestions and criticisms from them.

There was also an Executive Board of nine, with a Chairman—elected in the same way as the Controlling Board—and they met about once in every ten days, and discussed the general workings of the community. Four times a year a General Meeting, which every worker was expected to attend, was convened.

Cases of misbehaviour amongst the Comrades were dealt with by a "Comradely Court" over which a Chairman presided. The Chairman was elected by vote; and the person on trial had the right of objection to any choice that he thought prejudicial to an impartial conduct of the case.

The penalties inflicted were usually fines of varying degrees. I asked what the alternatives were, but only received an evasive reply. I can believe that they were not pleasant. In the case of repeated offences by the same person a decree of expulsion from the Commune might be promulgated, but only on a majority vote of two-thirds.

The principal offences against the Commune were petty theft, bad or careless work, damage to farm property and refusal to work. There had once been a case, I was told, of a Comrade who "spoke bad against the Government" and this was considered so serious that his case was sent up to some higher court of appeal, quite outside the Commune, and eventually went to Moscow—the seat of Government.

"What happened after that, we do not know," said my informant. "He was taken away, and we heard nothing more."

To "speak bad against the Government" is the most serious offence that can be committed in the Soviet State, and it was not very difficult to guess why nothing more had been heard of the offender.

I thought of some of the expressions I had often heard applied to the unfortunate Government at home by sorely-tried taxpayers, and felt glad that neither the degree of sedition implied, nor the penalties involved, were on the Russian scale of magnitude.

The Comradely Courts were apparently very

popular and were always crowded with spectators.

The Commune ruling with regard to sexual offences was based on a conception of sexual morality widely removed from our own. No marriage regulations existed, and no registration of marriages took place. A man and a woman wishing to marry applied for married quarters (of which I shall have more to tell later) and received them.

Did they, I asked, usually remain together?

Sometimes they did, and sometimes they didn't. Those who had been already married before they arrived at the Commune were generally faithful to one another, especially where there were children.

The young people were often very promiscuous. They changed partners frequently.

What happened if a girl was left expecting a child by a man who had gone to live with another woman? I asked this question of the most intelligent woman in the Settlement—an Esthonian, who had lived for many years in the United States and spoke English, German and Russian fluently, and could make herself understood in French.

She answered with a shrug of the shoulders. It was right that a child should have a father and a mother, and it was right that a father should contribute towards the maintenance of his child. The girl could appeal to the Comradely Court, and the onus of proving that he was *not* the father of her child lay on the man.

Did this frequent re-shuffling of partners lead to quarrels and jealousies?

Apparently not.

There had only been one fight in twelve years, said the Esthonian, when a woman had thrown a bucket at another woman's head.

She seemed to think that on the whole everybody worked too hard and was too worn-out by the end of the day, to have any energy left for emotional violence.

It was also she who told me that the tall Armenian I had talked to on the night of my arrival—he was young, and very good-looking in a swarthy way — had been one of the worst offenders they had ever known, in the matter of promiscuity.

"He took nearly all of the girls behind the pig-house," said Eva, the Esthonian. "Not even a very nice place," she added thoughtfully.

As a matter of fact, the Armenian left the Commune two days after I came—but whether of his own free will or not, I never learnt.

There were a great many nationalities at the Commune. The majority of the Comrades were Russians, Ukrainians and Caucasians, and there were Poles, Finns, Armenians, Lithuanians, Latvians and one Chinaman. The Chinaman had married a Russian girl in the Commune.

Most of the so-called Americans were not American-born at all, although many of them had at one time or another taken American citizenship. They had nearly all come originally from middle-Europe, but they had lived and worked—or been out of work—for years in the States, and talked the worst and most debased form of "N'Yoick" English.

There had never been any English member of the Settlement. A young Englishman had come once and had stayed for a fortnight, and then he got ill and went away. They had never had any French members at all.

I asked about visitors.

At one time, foreign visitors had been sent out in cars from the nearest Tourist centre in the summer, to spend the day and inspect the farm. (I would lay any wager that they didn't inspect all of it.)

They had to have a special meal prepared for them, and they interrupted the work, and were generally considered to have been a nuisance. For several years now the Commune had had no outside visitors, and I somehow got the impression—but it was a vague one, founded on no specific information—that it was, or had been, in some disfavour with the Government.

At all events it was no longer used as a showplace for tourists.

I never really understood why I had been allowed to go there, and to remain as long as I did. I can only suppose it was due to my alleged acquaintance with the man whose name had been given me by the American—almost equally unknown to me—deputizing for my friend at the Embassy.

After the Secretary had shown me over the farm, he told me that dinner would be at eleven and begged me to go anywhere I liked and do anything I pleased.

"Be like home!" was his benevolent parting injunction.

I was not like home—far from it—but I was

[27]

grateful for his kindness—and indeed all the time I was there I met with kindness and friendliness from everybody.

That first morning was perhaps a little forlorn, but the sun was shining and it was gloriously hot, and I knew that the first few days are always the hardest. I walked about a great deal, and I sat in the sun, and watched a number of small children playing about in the alfalfa. Most of them wore dirty little cotton smocks, and the boys were in ragged shirts and trousers. Nearly all had shaven heads. It did not improve their appearance, but was a precaution against lice. Incidentally I never, at the Commune, caught anything worse than a flea—but I had a liberal supply of Keating's Powder with me, and dusted the bed and the bedroom and most of my clothes with it every night.

At about a quarter-past eleven a bell rang, and went on ringing for some while. I saw the workers making their way towards the canteen and I went up to an elderly man wearing horn-rimmed spectacles—which made me think he must have lived in America—and asked whether he could speak English.

He could. He was a Finn, and had been in California for several years.

We went in to dinner together, and I sat next him, and although he hardly spoke at all he was very kind, and when I asked whether it was possible to have a drink of water he went and fetched one for me. Actually, of course, I ought to have asked for water to wash in—Heaven knows I required it—but I had decided to go into the whole of that question thoroughly in the afternoon.

For dinner, a large tin bowl of cabbage soup stood in the middle of each table with an iron dipper beside it. Everybody helped themselves and ate from smaller tin bowls. There was a tin spoon and fork at each place, but no knife. A Comrade presently took away each soup-basin and put in its place a basin of stew.

The soup had been good, but the meat was very tough and quite tasteless. The Finn took a clasp-knife from his pocket to deal with it, but my other neighbours first speared their meat on their forks and then tore it apart with their teeth.

I had a very small penknife in my pocket, and brought it out, to everybody's great amusement. Several of the women held out their hands for the knife, and looked at it, and laughed a great deal,

[29]

and I laughed too, and we managed to exchange a few words in one language or another.

The remainder of the meal consisted of black bread. It was very good bread, and very well made. Milkless tea was in a huge jug.

Dinner, and in fact all the meals, were usually very silent, and the workers hardly ever lingered at their tables. They had an hour off at dinner-time and seemed to spend most of it either in sitting or walking about, doing nothing.

To finish here with the subject of the meals: the midday one always took place between eleven and half-past, and the next, and last one, at six. It was quite surprising how very quickly one got accustomed to the long intervals between. Supper was much the same as dinner: always soup, usually made with cabbage, but sometimes with beans or fragments of meat, and always unlimited quantities of bread. The second supper dish was sometimes macaroni, sometimes cheese made with sour milk, and sometimes fried eggs.

Except for the meat, nothing was badly cooked, and the tea, or barley-coffee, was always served hot. I found that my digestion stood up to it all better than I expected, although I had to give up eating the meat. My chief trouble was that, in the heat, I grew very thirsty between meals, and felt exceedingly doubtful about the water.

There was a little tap, outside the canteen that could be turned, when water — rather disconcertingly — spouted upwards instead of downwards, and it was said to be drinking-water. As everybody drank it and seemed none the worse, I decided to risk it, and suffered no bad results at all. But I am bound to say that it tasted very odd.

I may say here that I had purposely brought no extra provisions of any kind with me, since one of the objects of the expedition was to live as far as possible the same kind of life as did the workers— and I was quite surprised and pleased to find that I remained just as strong and well as ever on a diet that, to me, seemed both restricted and unpalatable. It was also almost entirely deficient in sugar, and I used to wonder whether anyone ever thought how bad it must be for the children. If so, I never heard it mentioned.

There were not, as may be supposed, many of the minor graces of civilization at the communal table. One took what one wanted, and left one's neighbours to look after themselves. A certain number of people ate with their fingers—not all. The worst trial, so far as I was concerned, was to see and hear the macaroni being dealt with on the opposite side of the table. . . . Macaroni is not, and never has been, the easiest thing in the world to eat gracefully, but there are degrees of horror connected with it, and I feel convinced that at the Commune we plumbed them all.

After the Finn and I had finished dinner, that first day—it took about ten minutes—I told him that I should be very grateful if he would either tell me, or find somebody else to tell me, what arrangements the Comrades had for washing purposes.

"Sure," he said.

He took me to one of the small houses that were dotted about. Behind a wire-netting door was a tiny dispensary, and at a table sat a very tall woman of about forty, with straight, short yellow hair and a strong, rather handsome face. This was the Esthonian woman, Eva, whose husband was the then Chairman of the Executive Board. They were both of them forceful and intelligent personalities, and I got to know Eva better than I did anyone else. In an absurd way, she always made me think

The worst trial was to see and hear the macaroni being dealt with on the opposite side of the table.

of Kipling's Mrs. Hawksbee. She was oddly hard and cynical on the surface, and fundamentally she was very kind.

She had a weak heart, and had no children.

The Finn, ushering me in, said, "I brought you English Comrade. She can visit with you awhile" —and departed.

Eva spoke English fluently, although with a strong accent, and I found that she, also, had lived in America a long while, and had a sister there, married to an American. The sister often sent her books and papers, but she said that hardly any of them ever reached her. She thought that they were confiscated at the post office.

Eva was a natural gardener, and had tried hard to make bulbs and seeds grow in front of her window, but the soil was too dry and heavy, and in the winter the cold was too severe. We talked about hyacinths, and I suggested that she should try and grow some indoors, and promised to send her some bulbs from England.

Then we entered upon the question of washing.

"Oh yes," said Eva, there was a wash-house, and she would take me to it at once.

"It is nothing to be proud about," she added

grimly. (Eva was the only Communist I ever met in Russia who was sometimes willing to admit that perfection had not, as yet, been achieved in every single direction under the new regime.)

The wash-house was a small brick building divided into two. In the first division, a wooden shelf ran round three walls and on the shelf stood tin pans and an occasional bucket. A barrel of water and a dipper stood near the door. The whole place was dripping and streaming with water, and the smell was indescribable.

This was the laundry, where the women washed their clothes. Most of them were half undressed, partly because of the heat and partly, I suppose, because they had no change of garment.

The inner division was the actual bath-house—and, by comparison, the laundry was a heaven of air and purity. The bath-house could be compared to nothing, except perhaps one's idea of the Black Hole of Calcutta.

It had no window, and was in consequence steeped in a holy gloom, like a Spanish cathedral, and the floor and the walls ran with water, and clouds of steam ascended from a big copper and came down again in the form of drips from the tiers of wooden steps against the wall.

Besides the copper, where the water was hot, there was a barrel of cold water and there were three or four long-handled iron dippers and several tin pans. The pans were communal. Only one or two of the women had buckets of their own.

When they went in to wash they left their clothes in the laundry, and there was always a Comrade in charge of them. Eva warned me there and then never to leave any of my belongings unwatched, never to take money or my watch to the wash-house, and to lock the door of my room every time I left it.

The Comrades, it is perhaps unnecessary to say, were as communal in the bath-house as they were everywhere else. I never went in there, for the purpose of fetching hot water, without finding several women, all stark naked, swilling themselves with water or standing about and talking. (Often they stood about without talking, for they were much more given to silence than to speech.)

Eva asked me if I would like her to lend me a bucket, and when I found that she had two, as well as an enamel basin — she seemed to be slightly ashamed of possessing so much private property—

[35]

I accepted.

I never felt able to join in the communal bath—mostly, I think, because I didn't care for the idea of leaving my clothes in the laundry while I had it —but I used to fetch hot water in Eva's bucket and carry it to my room, and wash there piecemeal.

Once, when it rained heavily, Eva said I must wash my hair, because the rain water was "better" —by which I think she meant softer, and probably cleaner.

On that occasion she lent me the enamel basin as well as the pail, for rinsing. So I obediently washed my hair, and most of my clothes as well.

All the time I was there I had my room, and the four beds, all to myself except for a very few days when an old woman who was ill was brought in. I could only hope that the illness was not smallpox. (Many of the workers were pitted with it.)

She was a Ukrainian, and could only speak her own language—and as a matter of fact I never heard her speak even that. She only groaned, quietly, whenever she was not asleep.

Sometimes I used to wonder if I should find her dead in the morning when the bell rang, for she never snored, or made a sound, except for the groans. But one day when I came back to the room in the middle of the day I found her gone, and was told that she had been taken to hospital.

There was a hospital, many kilometres away, and sick people who were thought to require an operation were jolted there, in one of the lorries, as a kind of last resort.

Accidents, illnesses and confinements at the Commune were all dealt with by Eva. She had had a certain amount of training—I think as a nurse— and the rest of her skill, such as it was, had been acquired, I suppose, from experience and from books. She was, as I have said, very intelligent— but her ideas of hygiene were non-existent.

I used to sit with her quite a lot in the dispensary, and I have seen her deal successively with a suppurating boil on a woman's arm, an injection administered to a child, and the reading of a clinical thermometer given to a malaria patient, all without the intervention of water, towel or disinfectant, and with hands that were far from clean to begin with.

Malaria was the most prevalent form of illness. Many of the workers got it regularly. Eva bemoaned the impossibility of obtaining quinine. She had once had a good supply of it, sent or brought from America, but the Soviet Government had since then imposed a prohibitive duty on the importation of quinine, and she was obliged to do without. She used instead a form of injection made up by herself, but she never told me of what it was composed. Her faith in her own injections was very great. Mine would have been greater if I had ever seen her sterilize a needle, and if I had not known that her entire pharmacopoeia only contained about a dozen little half-empty bottles and a pair of scales for the weighing of a white powder—I never knew what it was—that she dispensed as a purge.

I asked her if maternity cases ever had to go to hospital, and she said that once or twice, when she had felt certain that an abnormal confinement was impending, she had sent a woman there. Nearly always, she delivered them herself.

Did a doctor ever visit the Commune?

Yes, if it was considered necessary one could be telephoned to, and would come. Also, there was a visiting doctor who appeared at irregular intervals according to the state of the roads. (The roads were mostly tracks across the rough prairie-land, made impassable by mud in wet weather, and very often by snow in the winter.)

Eva, I think, was a little bit offended at my suggestion of a doctor. She told me rather curtly that when he did come he was principally occupied in dentistry. She herself, she added—perhaps rather sinisterly—had not strong enough wrists.

The only epidemics that had been known in the Commune in thirteen years were one of measles, which had been confined to the children, and a more or less annual visitation of influenza. It was not a severe form of influenza, and nobody had ever died of it.

It is only fair to add that nearly all the children looked very healthy and strong. They lived almost entirely in the open air, and there was a kind of day school for them to go to while their mothers were at work.

Eva took me to see the school. It was one of the best of the buildings, although the amount of floor space seemed terribly inadequate for something like fifty or sixty children, all under seven years of age.

Most of them set up a most frightful howling

at the sight of Eva, and she explained to me that they were afraid of her injections.

From this, and from what she told me at other times, I deduced that almost all of them were given injections on every possible occasion.

I asked if there were any tuberculosis amongst them. Whether Eva really understood what I meant by the word, or whether she simply was ignorant of the nature of tuberculosis, I cannot say—but her reply astonished me.

"Seventy-three per cent of the babies are tubercular," she glibly informed me. "I give them injections when they are babies, and then one more when they are eleven or twelve and by the time they are fifteen, or sixteen, they are all right."

The day school, which was really a crèche, was only for little children. The older ones, who were not allowed to work on the land and in the farm until the age of fourteen, ran very wild.

Eva asked me if I thought I could "discipline them." I said it would be difficult to discipline big children with the extremely inadequate amount of Russian at my command, but that I should like to help take care of the little ones—and later on I did so.

I have said that the children's crèche was one of the best of the buildings.

The housing problem, there as elsewhere in the Soviet Republic, was the most difficult one of all. Actually, it was clear to me that a wonderful amount had been achieved in a very few years. The original hut in which the pioneers had lived in 1922 still stood, but most of the houses built since then were of brick or lath-and-plaster. One or two were concrete. Each contained from four to six rooms, and one family lived in each room.

They were not large rooms: about 14 by 16 feet, and sometimes much less. A family might consist of a husband and wife, or of a husband and wife and two children, or even three. Nobody had more than three children, and most couples had only one. But whatever the size of the family, that one room had to serve them as a dwelling-place.

Unmarried girls over fourteen went to sleep, all together, in a Women's Dormitory, and the boys had a Men's Dormitory. They slept about twelve or fourteen in a room. It was hoped to build more accommodation as time went on, and judging from what has already been done in the past ten or twelve years, I have no doubt that this will be achieved. I went inside quite a number of the workers' rooms, and there were nearly always some rather pathetic little attempts at decoration and home-making.

One woman had put up a frail little pair of muslin curtains that she washed and ironed two or three times a week. She had brought them, three years earlier, from New York.

None of them had any possessions worth speaking of. A clock was a very rare object, and there were no pictures, excepting occasional photographs of friends or relations, and the usual coloured newspaper supplements featuring leaders of the Revolution. Except in Eva's home, I never saw any books or newspapers.

There was, however, a library behind the canteen, with a very few books in it, and some newspapers. Some of the men went there and looked at the papers in the evenings. They had a table there too, with a kind of game that looked like a cross between billiards on a reduced scale and Corinthian bagatelle on a large scale. It wasn't very much used when I was there—but then it was summertime. Perhaps it was more popular in the winter.

(4)

I found it quite difficult to induce anybody to let me do any work. At last I discovered that the simplest plan was to go up and join a group of workers and just do whatever they were doing.

That was how I came to work in the bakery.

The head baker was a very tall blue-eyed Pole. He always wore a chef's cap and a more-or-less white smock. He, also, had been in America.

He baked his bread in a huge brick oven, and it was always very good. Two of his assistants were women, one Polish and the other Russian, and they kneaded the dough with their knuckles, in a huge crock, for hours and hours. It seemed to me that even the most inexperienced person could hardly go wrong in so uncomplicated a rite, and I kneaded with them.

One of the women, called Anna, who was about fifty and had a nice, broad, smiling, freckled face, had achieved the distinction of having been married for eighteen years to an American and being still unable to speak or to understand one single word of English.

She talked to me in a Russian dialect, and when I failed to understand her, as I generally did, the other woman—Julia—translated.

Julia, was I think, about forty years old—perhaps less. She was a Pole, and so was her husband. They had been for years in America where Julia had worked in a silk-stocking factory, and the husband—she told me—had been out of work nearly all the time. (This was afterwards amplified by Eva, who explained that, in America, Julia's husband had been continually in and out of prison for promoting strikes and general Communistic propaganda. On coming to the Commune, he settled down into a most excellent worker, and never gave any trouble at all. I got to know him quite well—he was in charge of the cow-houses— and he was one of the nicest men in the settlement.)

Both Anna and Julia were very kind to me. They had a conviction, which nothing could shake, that I was very frail and delicate and ought not to be allowed to work. I think this was mostly founded on the fact that I weighed so much less than they did. All the women, almost without exception, were fat and heavy. Some of them asked me, via Julia, what they could do so as to become slim, and we held quite a little consultation about it. I suggested a few exercises, which made them laugh a great deal, and advised them to drink after, instead of during, meals.

Actually, I believe the chief reason why most of them were so heavy and shapeless was that they wore no belts or supports of any kind. But as I knew very well that such things were quite unobtainable it would have been of no use to mention them.

We often had long breaks in the middle of the morning's kneading, and nobody seemed to mind. Anna and Julia frequently implored me to sit down and rest, and they never allowed me to do the really heavy work of turning over the huge mass of dough in the crock. Anna, who was very muscular, would do it single-handed, but Julia could not.

The kneading was very monotonous work, and made the muscles of one's forearms ache, and sometimes for a change I used to do the rolling, with a wooden pin, and help Julia cut up the dough into strips afterwards.

The Polish baker often came in and talked to us, and so did the friends of Anna and Julia.

One day I gave an exhibition of everything that I had in my handbag (I always carried it about with me, after Eva's warning) and they were rather pathetically delighted, especially with a little pocket-mirror in a case. They snatched it and looked at themselves so eagerly that I suspected many of them of not having any looking-glass at all.

My powder-compact and lipstick were a great success, and they made me use both, then and there, and screamed with laughter at the result.

They all sniffed at a tiny bottle of smelling-salts, and shook their heads over it a good deal—I believe they thought it was the English idea of scent—but the greatest success of all was a pair of reading-glasses.

Each in turn tried them on, exactly like children, and I gave them my small pocket-calendar to show them how it magnified print. Exclamations of astonishment and delight resounded, and one or two of them were disappointed and surprised because the glasses would not magnify anything else.

Most of them also tried on my wrist-watch, and

seemed pleased with the effect.

It made one realize under what primitive conditions most of them had always lived. For women like Eva and Julia, who had known life in a much more civilized aspect, it must have been a difficult existence, especially at first.

I used to visit Julia in her own home—that is to say, the one room in which she and her husband lived. They had no children.

She showed me what was evidently her greatest treasure—a photograph-album. It was filled with snapshots of American friends, and with photographers' pictures — all taken in America — of wedding-groups. Her own wedding-group was there. Julia and her husband had been married in a church, and Julia had had her hair waved, and had worn a very frilly white frock and a wreath of flowers. I asked her if she regretted America, and she said: Often. During her first three years at the Commune she had hated being there, and had wanted all the time to go back. Now, she said, she was getting used to it. There were no worries. In America, she had continually been worried, about how to pay the rent, how to live, how to keep a job when she had one and how to get one when she hadn't. She admitted freely that she missed the shops and the amusements and social life, of her American days.

Then she told me about her old home in Poland. She had left it when she was only sixteen, and had never been back there since. She showed me a photograph of her family—a group of six brothers and one sister — herself — and their father and mother. Just before Julia left home her mother had had another baby—who was now a young woman in her twenties. The brothers were all married, and Julia had gone from the United States to see one of them in Canada.

The mother was dead.

It was Julia's great desire to get her young sister out to the Commune, but for two years she had had no letters, and thought that probably none of hers had reached home. She had sent a letter to friends in America, enclosing one addressed to her sister in Poland and had begged them to forward it, and to receive and send on the answer in the same way.

As far as I understood, the Polish authorities distrusted communications from the Soviet Republic, and probably confiscated them undelivered.

[48]

I VISIT THE SOVIETS

In Julia's room there was a double bed, with a coloured bedspread, a sewing-machine and an electric iron, and two rugs. All of them came from America. The two chairs, the table and a large wooden chest were Russian.

There was nothing else in the room.

It was most beautifully clean and tidy, always. There were four rooms in the house, with one family living in each. The little strip of ground under Julia's window belonged to her, and she had planted phlox there. They were the only flowers I saw in bloom at the Commune, except a little patch of red poppies cherished by Eva.

I often visited with Julia—she always made use of that expression—and she used to lend me her electric iron when I had been washing my clothes. She was always friendly and kind, and so was her husband.

Julia and Anna, and one or two of the other women, called me "Elisa"—the Russian diminutive of Elizabeth. Most of the others called me "Comrade Dashwood."

(5)

The door next to mine, No. 3, led into a room,

the same size as the one that I occupied, in which lived a family of four, husband and wife and two children of six and three years old.

The wife, whose nationality I never discovered, spoke to me sometimes in what I suppose was a Russian dialect, but I never could understand a word she said. She was a schoolmistress and held classes in the evenings. Most of the pupils were young men, and I think she was teaching them to read and write. This she did in the outer room, where there were a long table and plenty of space, and which was communal.

But in the day-time, when the door of No. 3 was left open for coolness, I used to see her struggling to keep the children quiet while her husband, who was ill, either lay on the bed looking very yellow, or sat, holding his head in his hands, at the table. Why the two little children did not go to the day school or crèche, I do not know. One day I invited the younger one into my room. He was a very merry, round-faced little creature, his bullet head completely shaven, and he was too young to be shy. His name was Mischa. Not only was Mischa enchanted to find himself in a strange room, but when I showed him the photograph of my own two children, he was highly amused. He went into fits and fits of laughter, and however often I showed him the photograph, it never failed to strike him as being inordinately funny.

The things he best liked to play with were a pair of light, coloured, steel shoe-trees, and the drinking-cup from the top of my thermos flask. He could amuse himself with them almost indefinitely, drawing imaginary water into the cup, and stirring it with the shoe-trees.

He talked to me a great deal, very earnestly, and seemed quite unaware that I never understood a word he said and took little or no part in the conversation. Perhaps he was like that heroine of Charlotte M. Yonge's who spent a happy afternoon with a little friend whom she never discovered to be deaf and dumb.

One day Mischa brought a friend with him, a little six-year-old girl called Xenia, who was very gentle and pretty and had been allowed to keep her hair on her head, although always tied up in a little white handkerchief.

Mischa gravely introduced her to the thermos cup and the shoe-trees and the other things with which he was in the habit of playing. Like a good showman, he kept his best effort for the end.

This was the photograph of the children.

Xenia laughed a good deal, but her amusement was as nothing to that of Mischa, who doubled himself up and positively shrieked with mirth.

He and Xenia played very happily and I always liked having them. It was less successful when Mischa's elder sister, Nadya, came too—after a good deal of coy peeping round the door, and running away, and coming back, and having to be persuaded.

She was a large, sturdy child, also with a shaven head, and she bullied Xenia successfully out of the room. She bullied Mischa too, but he held his ground—I suppose in honour of having been the first discoverer of the new playground. They were very obedient children, and never protested when I had to send them away, and they always of their own accord replaced everything they played with exactly where they had found it.

Their mother came and made me a long speech about them, which I guessed was to the effect that I was to send them away when I was tired of them, and I nodded and said Yes, yes, yes, and patted their shorn heads to indicate that I liked them—

as I did, especially Mischa.

They brought their toys to show me: a very old doll, a stuffed monkey and a few bricks.

All this was in wet weather—for we had several consecutive days of pouring rain, about which I shall tell later.

It was impossible not to suppose that it was a relief to that harassed-looking mother and the yellow husband, not to have their two small, active children shut up in a single room with them from morning till night, when it was too wet to turn them out of doors.

Sometimes I helped to look after the babies at the crèche, but I was unfortunately taken there by Eva in the first instance, and at the sight of Eva they all either burst into tears or screamed and tried to hide. She explained to me that they associated the sight of her with "injections"—she must have "injected" with reckless frequency — and presumably they felt that I might at any moment deal with them in the same way, for they would never really make friends with me.

My chief difficulty actually was to find sufficient occupation in a day that began at 5.15 and ended at 9.30 or 10.

I VISIT THE SOVIETS

Once or twice I helped in the kitchen—chiefly with the washing-up—and on several occasions I went out with the horse and waggon that carried dinner to the workers in the field. Most of them were women, and they were hoeing potatoes. It struck me that the crop was a poor one, and that the weeds were far more numerous than the potato plants. The corn, on the other hand, looked splendid and was already standing two feet high, early in June.

Since the Soviet system has abolished the days of the week—so that one felt guilty of a positive impropriety if one accidentally referred to "Monday" or "Sunday" by their names—each sixth day is, theoretically, a rest-day. On the farm, rest-days were extremely sparse in the summer, and only too numerous in the bad weather. Most of the workers only worked in eight- or nine-hour shifts. Their leisure time, as far as I could see, was spent in sitting, lying or walking about in complete silence.

At intervals, when the state of the roads was favourable, a travelling cinema came to the farm. It was announced for 8 o'clock, and usually arrived at 9.30 and started any time after 10. It struck me that the Comrades were only moderately enthusiastic about the films. The projection was bad, and the pictures were usually out-of-date Hollywood.

Nearly every evening after supper—no meal at the Commune ever took me more than ten minutes, from start to finish—I used to go over to the cowhouse and watch the cows being milked—partly because the sounds and scents of the yard were what the kind little Secretary would have called "being like home."

A young woman who was head of the milking department used to come, with her small daughter of two, and sit with me and talk to me. She was one of the very few good-looking women I saw in Russia—tall, and with curling golden hair, and she had not yet put on weight.

When any of the Comrades referred to her, in speaking to me in English, they called her "the cow-lady," just as they called Julia "the bread-lady" and the hoeing-brigade "the field-ladies." I think they took the word "lady" to be an equivalent of "citizeness," because I once heard myself called "Lady Dashwood" by Eva's husband, and I am sure he would never willingly have thrust me into the titled classes.

[55]

The cows were driven into their stalls, each one having her head through a wooden halter, and milked into buckets. The buckets, alas, were dirty, and so were the hands of the milkers. I soon ceased to regret that I never saw any of the children drinking milk.

Julia's husband was employed in the stock-yard and he often took me to see the bulls and the calves. The calves, even in that hot June weather, were kept in pens in the stables until they were ten or twelve weeks old. They were never with their mothers at all, but were fed out of pails from the very beginning.

All the live-stock had to be given fodder, all the year round, because there was so little grazing for them in the fields.

As for the horses, they were very fine animals, and I never saw them do any work at all except drawing an occasional load of straw, or a waggon with dinner for the workers in the fields.

They were nearly all bred and kept for the Red Army, and a young Comrade used to exercise them madly up and down the fields, watched by an admiring—and probably envious—group of young men.

The young men, incidentally, possessed a football. I never saw them play an organized game with it, but they used to kick it about sometimes, without very much enthusiasm.

(6)

One night there was a thunderstorm, and I heard the rain coming down in torrents. In the morning it was still coming down in torrents, and the state of the ground outside was indescribable. Ponds two and three feet deep had appeared, and the mud was like black glue into which one sank ankle-deep.

Huge iron scrapers and pointed sticks were placed at the door of the canteen—but even so, most people took their boots off before going inside.

The stout country shoes that I had thought myself sensible for bringing with me were about as useful as a pair of ballroom slippers might have been. Even in the few yards from my room to the canteen they were nearly sucked off my feet a dozen times, and I must have scraped and poked and kicked quite a pound of wet mud off each of them.

In the course of the morning there came a knock at my door, and a peasant woman, smiling broadly, handed me a huge pair of gunboots, an oilskin and a pair of large white cotton socks. There was also a note:

COMRADE DASHWOOD

Am lending you a raincoat, pair of rubber boots and pair of socks. Don't think I am doing this from humanitarian point of view — am doing this because am afraid you'll get sick and I wouldn't be capable of taking care of you.

EVA S.

Whatever Eva's motives — and I feel sure they were thoroughly "humanitarian"—I accepted her kindness thankfully, although the boots were extraordinarily uncomfortable and I walked in them very awkwardly, and rubbed a sore place on one ankle.

The rain went on, with hardly an intermission, for three days and nights and I began to wonder whether we should soon begin to think about building an Ark. All the work in the fields was stopped, and the days were "rest-days" whether the workers wished for them or not. My immediate neighbours congregated in the big communal room just outside my door and turned on a loud-speaker that seemed only capable of transmitting a loud, dreary kind of Russianized jazz. There was one tune in particular, that recurred with extraordinary frequency, which always began as if it was the "Song of the Volga Boatmen," and always turned into something else about the fourth bar.

I had brought only one book with me, and at this stage I recklessly increased my allowance of five pages per day, to one chapter. I had always wanted to find out if one *could* do without reading at all, and am bound to admit that in my case one couldn't. On the other hand, I quite triumphed over cigarette-smoking, and never smoked once the whole time I was in Russia. At the Commune none of the women smoked, and very few of the men.

The rain was very much needed on the land, and I felt a bit like Mrs. Gummidge in minding it more than anybody else did. But there really was very little to do when it was impossible to stay out of doors a moment longer than was absolutely necessary.

However I managed to visit with Eva, more than once.

Her intelligence impressed me more than that of anyone I met in the Soviet Union.

She was a convinced Communist, but, unlike most convinced Communists, was quite willing to admit the existence of another point of view, and she would also admit that the new régime in the U.S.S.R. was still capable of improvement.

She asked me a number of questions about England, especially the position of women there, and suggested that I should give a talk one evening to the Comrades, which she would translate.

"I guess it won't be the first time you've stood up on a platform and talked," she remarked, looking me up and down with a mixture of shrewdness and amusement.

I admitted that she was right, and told her I was a writer, and she said she'd guessed *that* all right, long ago.

It was not easy to make Eva talk about herself, and I never learnt her story, much as I should have liked to do so. The most revealing thing she ever said was one day when I took out my fountain-pen in order to write down her full address.

"You gotta pen, have you? I thought I'd 'a gone crazy for mine, to start with—but I don't never think about it now. You get used to anything, with time."

We talked once about religion—banished from the Soviet State. It was obvious that Eva was in favour of its abolition, but there again she was much less intolerant than most of the people with whom I had spoken.

"You can't take it away from the old people," she admitted. "They've always believed, and I guess they always will. Sometimes they say to us, 'God'll punish you for what you are doing, see if He don't.' "

"Can't they ever get any religious services at all?"

She shook her head.

"There was a church once, not far from here, but it had been shut up a long time, even when we came. It's been pulled down now, and they're using some of it for the farm buildings."

It was true. I had seen some pieces of heavily-gilt moulding in the carpenter's shop, and a panel of wood with a painting on it of the Madonna.

"I guess nobody don't hinder them saying their prayers all they want," said Eva, "but that's about all they've got left of it."

[61]

She had a curiously dry, matter-of-fact way of speaking, even about things on which she evidently felt strongly, and she was one of the clearest thinkers I have ever met.

"Sure, everybody won't never be equal, or stay equal," she admitted, in talking about Socialism. "I guess personality's always going to count. Some people'll get to the top, and others'll stay at the bottom. All the Communism in the world ain't goin' to make human nature different. What it does, is to give every feller his chanst."

So far as personality was concerned, it was evident enough that Eva's own strong personality had given her a leading position at the Commune. But she had no sort of precedence over anybody else, and all the comrades alike called her either "Eva" or "Comrade Eva."

She had a sense of humour and, still more unusual, a sense of satire—a quality seldom found in primitive surroundings.

Any form of artificiality she disliked and distrusted. I once said to her politely that I hoped I wasn't staying too long in her house, and keeping her from other business—to which she replied sardonically, "If you were, I guess I'd have said so.

I'm not so gentle as all that."

It was she, also, who when we were taking an evening walk together near a swamp, thoughtfully remarked that there was a very bad smell about —which there certainly was—and the only other place she'd noticed it was at the supper-table whenever salad was served.

(7)

I regretted very much that I had taken no camera with me to the Commune. There are so many restrictions for travellers in the U.S.S.R. as to the taking and developing of photographs that I had thought it would be useless.

Actually, on the farm, I could certainly have photographed anything and everyone without any interference. My credentials were never questioned, and nobody so much as asked if I had a passport at all. I could, I am perfectly certain, have stayed on there for months.

It was neither the discomforts—to which one became quickly accustomed—nor the monotony, nor the rather trying lack of privacy, that sent me away in the end. Still less was it, as some of my

[63]

relations had hopefully suggested to me before I left England, that my health was unequal to the strain of a few unaccustomed privations. My health remained, on the contrary, excellent.

It was, oddly enough, a calamity that I had not foreseen. I got toothache.

I used to think that I could have borne a severe illness much more heroically.

There was something so hopeless about having a toothache, that might at any moment become much worse—and that seemed to me quite bad enough already—and I had nothing with me to try and relieve it, except aspirin.

The thought of the visiting doctor with strong wrists filled me with only less horror than did the thought of Eva, and in fact I was so terrified at the mere idea of Eva's ministrations, which would certainly have taken the form of an injection, that I never said a word about the toothache, to her or to anybody else.

I made my arrangements for leaving—they had to be altered a good many times, because of persistent rain which made the roads impassable even for the motor-lorries—and Eva arranged a party in the canteen, for the night before my departure.

And I may here say that, driven nearly to desperation, I suddenly remembered a bottle of iodine solution in my bag, and painted the whole of one side of my mouth with it lavishly, and either that, or the prospect of going into comparative civilization again, actually did put an end to my toothache for the time being.

The party was announced for 8.30, and by some miracle of punctuality began only an hour later.

The Comrades sat at the little tables in groups of four or five—it was like a kind of skeleton *café chantant*, without glamour, music, drinks or excitement. It was not without beauty, because several of the faces, especially the older ones, were individually very fine. But the whole effect was curiously drab, even though most of the women had put on their best dresses for the occasion.

I sat at a table with a particularly hard-boiled Comrade who had originally come from the middle of the Balkans but had spent most of his life in the United States, and I remember that he raised a laugh by telling me that in America he had had two very good homes and two sets of "folks."

"And I didn't never marry either," he added

[65]

triumphantly.

One learnt not to ask the men what had brought them to the Commune.

I suppose a similar discretion prevails in Foreign Legion circles.

Not that I mean that there was any particularly discreditable story attached to any of them, but a good many had certainly been political agitators in other countries, and would no doubt have found difficulty in returning there, had they wished to do so.

When the evening's entertainment at last began it reminded me in the most absurd way of a Village Social at home.

Eva's husband was the Chairman, and he made a short speech, first in Russian and then in English, opening the proceedings and announcing the items.

The Comrade from England—myself—would give a short talk and answer any questions about England and English affairs, Comrade Eva would translate, and there would then be a concert.

The "Comrade from England" then went and stood beside the little table on the stage, feeling exactly as if about to address a Women's Institute or a Mothers' Union at home, and spoke.

They were a very good audience, perfectly silent and attentive, although not more than one-third could have understood a word I was saying.

In my speech I told them that the Soviet experiment was regarded with interest in England, and that my own village, and one or two neighbouring ones, had made me promise to come on my return and tell them all about my visit to Russia.

I said how favourably I had been impressed with the facilities given to women workers in the U.S.S.R., with the care taken of the children of workers, and with the institution known as "Bolshevo" just outside Moscow (a colony for young offenders, not quite unlike Borstal but with far more freedom.)

I was also very glad to take the opportunity of saying how much struck I was with the universal kindness and courtesy shown to foreigners, by Russians. I had gone about by myself a great deal, and had lost my way with all the thoroughness and frequency of a person devoid of any sense of direction, and again and again had benevolent Russian strangers gone miles and miles out of their way solely in order to conduct me to my destination. And they had listened to my halting Russian, not only with grave courtesy, but with sufficient intelligence to make out what it was all about.

Then I told them a little about agricultural methods in the West of England, and about village life—carefully avoiding the fatal words, "capitalist system" which I knew well were in every mind.

Everywhere I had been in the U.S.S.R. I had found that the faintest hint of criticism was not so much resented as looked upon as the unfounded mutterings of jealousy and ignorance—but I saw no reason, on this occasion, for abstaining from it altogether. So I told the Comrades that, much as I admired many of their institutions for children, I regretted the attempt to submerge all individuality, and felt strongly that, whilst herd life might be admirably suited to the majority, it would never succeed in producing the creative artist.

I ended, of course, by thanking them for all their kindness to me and by telling them, as I honestly could, that I should always be glad of my experiences amongst them.

Eva translated what I had said, and I could follow her Russian well enough to know that the translation was full and accurate. She had been taking notes all the time.

The audience applauded us both, and was invited to ask questions.

The questions were innumerable, and many of them demanded facts and figures that I was quite unable to supply.

What was the opinion of the English nation as a whole about the Abyssinian war?

What were the unemployment figures in 1936 as compared with those of 1935?

(The words "Capitalist System" almost seemed to form in the air in letters of fire, and I said that—whilst unable to furnish exact figures—I could assure them that the unemployment total had lessened. God forgive me! I hope it was true.)

How was King Edward?

Splendid, I replied heartily, and quite as though I had heard from him that morning.

What was thought of Romain Rolland in England?

Of Germany?

Of abortion?

This last topic of conversation was as prevalent everywhere I went in Russia, as is that of the

[69]

weather in England. A tram conductor in Rostov, punching my ticket, enquired my views on the subject. When I was at the Commune, a law to repeal the legalization of abortion was under discussion. But in any case I think the Russians found it an interesting subject, well calculated to promote the social amenities.

I was also asked several question all bearing on the position of the English working woman. Nearly all the questions were intelligent ones, and showed a vital interest in the problems of the present-day world.

One Comrade—I thought a little aggressively— demanded point-blank which way Comrade Dashwood intended to vote, when the Revolution reached England. I am nearly certain that he said *"when,"* and that Eva translated it as *"if."*

At all events, I briefly replied that a Revolution in England, if there ever was one, would not take the same form as a Revolution in Russia. The Communist party, I said firmly, was negligible, and my own sympathies, personally, were with the Labour party.

Eva, with a diplomatic skill that I was able to appreciate, translated the first part of this sentence as I had spoken it: omitted my slighting reference to the Communist party altogether, and rendered the words "Labour party" as "the workers." Since the whole of Soviet Russia now consists of "the workers," the natural result was that I was understood to have declared myself an enthusiastic supporter of Communism, and was heartily applauded.

After that came the concert.

The stage, to my surprise, had a very good drop-scene and back-cloth, both well painted. I asked who had done them, and Eva said that "an artist" had once visited the Commune, but had only stayed a very short time.

The entertainment was nearly all provided by the Ukrainians. About twelve men and women, all wearing national costume, came in and sang. It was very pathetic to see the gay red-silk skirts and beautiful embroidered aprons and wreaths of artificial flowers, so carefully kept and so seldom worn, and so unlikely ever to return to the lands from whence they had been brought.

The songs were part-songs, sung in a minor key and very, very slowly. There was no accompaniment and the singers kept wonderfully in tune and, so far as I could trust my ear, did not end up by singing flat. But the songs were of incredible length.

"They are very nice," said Eva despondently in my ear, "but they have no end."

It sometimes almost seemed as though they hadn't.

They sang several times, and one couple danced —a very attractive peasant dance. Then they all danced a "wedding-dance" with a pair in the middle, and all the others joining hands in a ring round them.

(I thought of Meg's wedding in *Little Women*, and Aunt March prancing with old Mr. Lawrence.)

Then there was some balalaika-playing by two Russian boys—but they were not very good—and one or two more songs.

Finally the Ukrainians, obviously feeling that they had not taken all the trouble of dressing themselves up for nothing, took possession of the stage again and sung more, and even longer, part-songs. Although they were too long, they really were effective in a strange, plaintive way.

Just before midnight the electric light—which

[72]

One couple danced—a very attractive peasant dance.

was made on the estate—gave its three customary warning flickers, and the meeting broke up.

So strongly did the atmosphere suggest a village meeting at home that I found myself positively expecting the familiar strains of "God Save the King." Needless to say, they were not forthcoming —and neither was the "Internationale."

When I went outside, the rain had stopped, and the sky was clear. I was to start early next morning, and said goodbye to most of my friends before I went to my room.

The Comrades were so exhilarated by their night's entertainment that they remained out of doors, singing what they remembered of the Ukrainian choruses whilst somebody twanged a balalaika, for what seemed to me like several hours afterwards.

(8)

I had naturally asked the Secretary to make whatever arrangements were least inconvenient to himself for sending me back to Rostov. Having by this time had some experience of travelling in Russia, I was not surprised when he asked me to

be ready at 5 o'clock in the morning. The road to
the station being still impassable, he had made a
very kind, though really unnecessary, arrangement
by which I was to be escorted to a light railway on
the estate, whence a little workmen's train would
take me—and the escort—to join the Rostov train
further down the line. The escort—one Comrade
David—was to take my ticket for me and see me
off.

I could perfectly well have done all this by myself, but I think Comrade David wanted the out-
ing. He was a dark-skinned, elderly man — and
whatever his name may have been, his origin was
neither Welsh nor English. Perhaps it was Hebraic.

Such was his zeal that he came and knocked on
my door in the morning, soon after 4 o'clock.

We had breakfast in the canteen before starting
—barley-coffee, black bread and fried eggs. The
canteen was open all night, as there were a number
of night watchmen always on duty.

Eva came and sat with me during breakfast,
and I think was sorry to see me go. I gave her
the only book I had with me, and she asked me
to put her name in it, and I promised to write to
her from England and to try and send her some

bulbs.

Then I shook hands with her and with the Secretary, and Comrade David and I climbed into the motor-lorry.

It jolted away over the prairie, dodging enormous ruts and plunging in and out of gigantic pot-holes, and every now and then skidding on the black slippery mud, or threatening to stick there altogether.

The last hundred yards or so we had to get out and walk. Comrade David, regardless of the fact that in the Soviet Union men and women are equal, insisted upon carrying my bag. He treated me not only with courtesy, but as though I were a particularly fragile piece of china.

At the little halt—where there was no station or platform, only the railway track and one cottage—we waited for some time, as one so frequently does in Russia. After a long while the tiny train appeared, with two wooden coaches in which sat the early workers.

Comrade David enlivened the journey by telling me that he was Ukrainian-born and had gone to Canada at the age of sixteen. Having done well there as an engineer, he had saved several thousand dollars and decided to travel. He placed nearly all the money in a Canadian bank, with instructions that it was to be sent to his parents in Ukrainia if he was not heard of within three years.

He then went to the States, found work there, and—like my Balkan friend of the night before—formed a home there, without hampering himself by any legal ties.

It was not until nearly five years later that he remembered his instructions to the Canadian bank.

He laughed heartily over the story, and assured me that he had never taken any further steps about his savings. He supposed that they had been duly sent to his father and mother, and that they believed him dead.

He had not heard from any of them for more than twenty years.

Some day, he said casually, he might go back to the village where he was born. He thought that it would be very funny, to surprise all the people who believed he was dead.

It had apparently not occurred to him that there might be very few left to surprise.

When we got to the station Comrade David

established me in a fly-blown little refreshment bar with strict instructions not to leave my luggage unwatched for a moment, and I gave him my purse and he went and got my ticket.

He stayed till the train went, and lifted in my bag for me, and I heard him giving the guard careful injunctions to see that I got out at Rostov. Then he shook hands with me and we parted.

I went, as I had come, "hard" class. This only means that the seats are of wood, and the sleeping-berths also wood of course are placed one above another, to the number of three. The coach is one long one, instead of being divided into compartments as in "soft" class, and by paying a few extra roubles a clean sheet and a hard pillow can be obtained. Comrade David had seen fit to order these additional comforts for me, although it was only a seven-hour journey and I should certainly never have thought of getting them for myself. But when they came, I lay down full length and slept.

The only serious drawback that I could see to travelling "hard" was the amount of spitting and throat-clearing that seems to go on all the time. Certainly, one caught an occasional flea—but then one was equally liable to do that in the best hotel

[77]

in Moscow.

Arrived in Rostov again—and feeling as though a whole strange lifetime had elapsed since I left it—I went back to the Intourist hotel where I had left my luggage in store. I had not thought of it before as being a palace of luxury—but it seemed so then, when I had a hot bath, and was given chicken and ice-cream for dinner, and eventually got into a bed that seemed quite incredibly soft!

The Intourist guides asked me a number of questions about the Commune, and seemed slightly awed at the thought of my having gone there at all, let alone remained there—and they particularly asked me, in so many words, not to encourage any other tourists to demand the same privilege, as it would certainly not be granted to them.

Afterwards, I visited — as a tourist and conducted with a party, by interpreters—several other farms, both Collective and State, in the neighbourhood of Rostov and that of Odessa. They were all "show" places—probably very interesting to the agricultural specialist, but giving no real insight into the lives and minds of the people working there.

I do not suppose that the Seattle Commune was

typical either: indeed, I know it was not.

It is very difficult to crystallize one's impressions into a few words—but mine, I think, were something as follows:

The chief drawbacks to life in the Commune were the utter lack of any privacy, the reversion to comparatively uncivilized standards of living, and the deadening effect of it all on individual development, both emotional and intellectual.

That an extraordinary degree of what, in a town, would be called "civic pride" flourished there, was undeniable. It is true, too—though surprising—that the standard of health was reasonably high.

Of the people there I can only say, from my limited experience, that they were kind, friendly and very hard-working.

Back again in another world, it is difficult to realize that such a place as the Seattle Commune exists, and is still going on, just as when I was living there.

THE NEW MRS. TROLLOPE

(1)

"YOU WILL," SAID MY AMERICAN PUB-
lisher, "get a humorous slant on Russia."

But shall I?

Do I even want to?

I think it would have chimed in better with my
own feelings if he had said something about my
leading a forlorn hope, or blazing a new trail. I so
little want to go and be humorous about Russia
that I can only get myself there at all by paying
all my expenses beforehand and knowing that I
shall never get them back again—and, once I've
actually started, by reminding myself continually
of Mrs. Trollope.

One has always felt a certain affinity with the
mother of Anthony Trollope. One's financial position, all too frequently, has approximated closely
to hers . . . one's efforts (less desperate and heroic
than hers, but prompted by a similar urgency and
of a similarly recurrent nature) and the eventual
value to literature and to posterity of efforts so
engendered, have always seemed to me to be very

much on a level with those of Mrs. Trollope.

Besides, I *like* Mrs. Trollope—"that battered but indomitable lady," as Michael Sadleir so admirably describes her.

Mrs. Trollope, when she went to America with innumerable pincushions and vases to start a Bazaar, was older than I am when I reluctantly set sail for Russia. She had had an incredible number of children, some of whom were left behind in circumstances of which the very thought must have made her feel wretched and some of whom came with her, which, in its way, was no doubt equally productive of wretchedness. What Mrs. Trollope may have lacked in actual practical organizing ability she more than made up for in courage and endurance.

Besides, she never pitied herself, unlike Mrs. Oliphant, whom I have never much liked, or even Jane Welch Carlyle, whom I love, but who had her moments of self-dramatization.

I can only endure the idea of going to Russia for three months by thinking continually of Mrs. Trollope going to America—and of Mark Tapley, arriving and remaining there.

I shall be the new Mrs. Trollope.

[81]

I VISIT THE SOVIETS

"You will enjoy," says one of my many little handbooks about the U.S.S.R., "the freedom and gaiety of life on board a Rusian ship, the camaraderie that prevails between the ship's officers, the crew and the passengers."

Very well, I get ready to enjoy it. I visualize us —Captain, crew, passengers and all—sitting together on the lower deck, singing the Song of the Volga Boatmen. They will sing, and we shall listen, and presently we shall sing, and they will listen.

I cannot make up my mind whether I shall give them "Annie Laurie" or "Sweet Lass of Richmond Hill"—which I believe was written in allusion to some fleeting fancy of King George the Fourth's. (If I tell them that, will they admire King George the Fourth for being democratic, or condemn him for being licentious? Perhaps better leave out any historical footnotes altogether.) But it turns out that the handbook is entirely mistaken—at least so far as this particular Russian ship is concerned.

We never set eyes on the Captain at all, and the crew though sometimes—not often—visible, sing no songs and utter hardly any words. They sit about a good deal, and they paint isolated bits of the ship—selected, apparently, out of mere caprice—and some of them are women. There is nothing else to remark about them. They display no *camaraderie*, even amongst themselves.

The passengers, it seems to me, set them no good example in this respect, even though the first and the tourist class have been democratically mixed up together for meals. We talk, but without *abandon*, and with a strong tendency to sort ourselves into exclusive groups—English, American, Russian and Balkan.

The English talk, very tepidly, about the weather and the countries to which they have, or have not, been. The Americans talk about sociology, and communism, and religion, and love, and food. The Balkans talk only about food.

No one, excepting themselves, knows what the Russians talk about. Anyway, there are only two of them, and they speak very little.

The new Mrs. Trollope spends a great deal of time in her cabin, feeling terribly homesick, and quite unable to envisage a humorous slant on anything at all.

Besides, *Bleak House* was a bad choice as a travelling-book. In spite of Mrs. Jellaby and Africa it is all much too sad, and I weep over the death of Rick—which even I have never done before—and sink into a deep depression on behalf of Sir Leicester Dedlock.

The American communist-in-chief, who says that her name is Mrs. Pansy Baker, asks me once what I am reading.

"Dickens."

"Dickens?"

She sounds so incredulous that I silently show her the cover of the book.

"Oh, my, oh my!"

She smiles and shakes her head, either in admiration or in despair.

I think it must be despair, because later on she enquires whether Englishwomen ever take any interest in the great political and sociological questions of the day.

I look round at my fellow-countrywomen, sitting on deck.

Two are knitting, speechlessly, and have been doing so for hours.

Two quite young ones, travelling together, are talking spasmodically about Airedale terriers.

One—myself—is reading Dickens.

[84]

One more—rather old—is asleep.

Mrs. Pansy Baker has not only been talking practically all day long—mostly about the great political and sociological questions of the day—she has also been learning Russian from one of the Russians and teaching him English in return, and reading in a large book called *Metaphysical Ideology*, vol. 2, and doing a little piece of embroidery— all at one and the same time.

No wonder she finds us, as she so frankly says, wanting in vitality, uplift, culture and the wider outlook.

I suggest to her that perhaps Russia will bring out our better selves.

"What is taking you to Russia, anyway?"

I can't say that one of her own compatriots has desired me to go to Russia in order that I may be funny about it. She'd never believe it. Mrs. Pansy Baker views Russia as a kind of Mecca—though not, naturally, in any religious sense—and from what I saw of myself in the glass this morning I don't look like a person who could be at all funny about anything. So I reply, very faintly, that I just thought it would be interesting, and feel that Mrs. Pansy Baker is really justified when she again shakes her head and says that Englishwomen just don't seem to know the meaning of enthusiasm.

I feel myself looking at her in an apathetic, and yet interested, way.

What a good-looking woman she is!

She must be nearly fifty, but she is slim, and with a bright, fresh colour, and always alert and interested, and she has large, light-brown eyes and pretty grey hair with darker streaks in it. Her clothes are charming.

Her teeth are admirable.

She comes from the Middle West and is a teacher—perhaps of Sociological Ideology?—and she has a husband, a son and a daughter.

She is, apparently, interested in everything in the world—but most of all in Communism, Psychology, Ethics, Philosophy, Sociology and the coming World Revolution.

She has much to say about all of them, and quotes the writings of one Professor Tod Mosher, whom she asserts to be the greatest living thinker in the whole of the United States.

It is not Mrs. Pansy Baker's fault that there is so little *rapprochement* between the Soviet crew and the passengers. She goes to the lower deck and runs about amongst them, and seems disappointed when, owing to their absence of English and her absence of Russian, no very serious contacts can be achieved.

She also, there or elsewhere, catches a flea, and is disturbed about it and talks of it so much that it presently acquires the status of a kind of illness.

"How is your Flea this morning, Mrs. Baker?"

"Well, I think the swelling has gone down some, but I'd be wiser to keep my leg still. I do wish I knew just what to do for it."

"Try Keatings in your cabin."

"Try white iodine ointment."

"Try ammonia."

"I'm afraid I didn't bring anything of that kind with me. Nothing like this has ever happened to me before," says Mrs. Pansy Baker.

It seems only kind to warn her that it will almost certainly happen to her again, travelling in Russia. But at this she shakes her head and looks very much surprised, and says that on the contrary, a very high grade of cleanliness prevails all over the Soviet State.

I can see that she really believes the Flea to be a British flea that came on at London Docks.

I VISIT THE SOVIETS

The two young Englishwomen, Miss Blake and Miss Bolton, offer to come to her cabin and catch it for her with a piece of soap. Perhaps they think it will be more amenable to its compatriots.

"Did you catch Mrs. Baker's Flea for her?"

"No. We couldn't see it."

"We turned out everything. We could see the marks where it *had* been. But nothing else."

How like a detective story it sounds.

But Miss Blake and Miss Bolton would make bad detectives.

They are large, heavy-footed young English-women, and although not related to one another look to me very much alike. Both of them are fair, with pink and white complexions, mouths always slightly ajar, and dressed in the same style of pink knitted jumper and tweed skirt.

One of them is almoner in a London Hospital, the other is Secretary to a Charity Organization. They share a flat in Campden Hill, and take their holidays together, and sit next to one another at meals, and on deck, and are never spoken of as two separate entities but always collectively, as Miss-Blake-and-Miss-Bolton.

There is also a Canadian on board—an engineer

—and he talks to Miss Blake and Miss Bolton, but doesn't like Mrs. Pansy Baker. When he asks after her Flea it is with a malignant air of satisfaction, and he puts forward a suggestion that it isn't a flea, but something worse.

I think the conversation has sunk to a very low level, and retire into the pages of *Bleak House* once more, but find that I am thinking about the next meal, and wondering what it'll be like.

(2)

The first sight of Leningrad completely reconciles me to having to call it Leningrad. Hitherto, I have romantically reflected on St. Petersburg, and all that one has ever read about a brilliant and picturesque thoroughfare called the Nevsky Prospekt. But when the ship enters the port and docks there, I see that there is no St. Petersburg any more—probably no Nevsky Prospekt either —and I am quite prepared to call it Leningrad, or anything else.

Grey buildings, off which the paint has flaked and never been renewed . . . and some forlorn-looking men standing about in very shabby coats and moulting fur caps . . . and bits of straw and paper whirling about in a cold wind—and mouldered iron gratings.

We are all herded through various sheds, and our suit-cases looked at and opened and turned inside out—and also repacked by the Customs officials, which is considerate—and our passports and money examined, and there is a very great deal of sitting about and waiting for nothing visible. It is very cold.

At last a motor-car takes away the first-class passengers, and an inferior kind of bus is indicated to the third-class tourists, of whom I am now one. I don't think this is a very good way for a Socialist country to behave. Surely it ought to receive all its visitors alike?

One Armenian, one Russian, the Canadian, Mrs. Pansy Baker and myself, with all the suit-cases on our feet, are rattled away over the cobbles and through the streets of Leningrad. They make a sad show.

The structure of many of the buildings is lovely, but most of them are falling down and all are in need of paint. Something—something rather gay and full of colour to which one has become accustomed—is missing.

There are no shops.

There is scarcely any traffic either, although as we approach the middle of the town there are trams, small, dirty, rattling trams that are crammed with people.

The pavements, like the trams, are thronged.

"Isn't it wonderful, to see all those folk walking along, like they had an object, instead of just hanging around street corners?" Mrs. Pansy Baker carols.

A very unoriginal sentiment. All the little books about Russia, and even the Intourist advertisements, have prepared me for this phenomenon, and I feel convinced that Mrs. Pansy Baker would have found some equally exhilarating quality in the sight of the pedestrians of Leningrad if they had all been on their way to the scaffold.

For my part, I don't find them exhilarating at all. They look grey, and shabby and poor — like the buildings, except that they lack the beauty and dignity of the buildings.

"To think I really am in Soviet Russia at last— why, it just seems like a wonderful dream. I guess you don't feel that way?" Mrs. Pansy Baker says

—and it is to her credit that she says it compassionately rather than indignantly.

I have to admit that I don't.

"Maybe you're tired."

I can't, and don't, tell her that I keep on thinking of the White Russians, and of how many were murdered, and how many exiled, and how many are still living — Heaven knows how — without home, without country, without hope.

Leningrad has plunged me into the deepest depression, and I wish I hadn't come.

Mrs. Trollope would never have given way like this at such an early stage.

I rally at the thought of Mrs. Trollope and say something spirited to the effect that I think we are now crossing the Neva.

(Rasputin—being put under the ice. But I keep to myself what I remember about that terrific and dramatic Nemesis.)

The hotel, when we reach it, is a large unattractive building, with purple-red paint peeling off it. Inside the hall it is full of Comrades, all standing about, all doing nothing. Then this is probably the Soviet equivalent of the street-corners?

The pavements, like the trams, are thronged.

I VISIT THE SOVIETS

Intourist sits behind a counter. Intourist is young, female, shabby in a faded jumper and badly fitting skirt, and with an authoritative manner.

"You will be together in one room."

It is Mrs. Pansy Baker and I who are to be thrust into this unwelcome proximity.

I ask, in French — which I hope she doesn't understand — if I can't have a single room. I can hear Mrs. Pansy Baker, also in lowered tones, pleading to the same effect in English.

Intourist, with no delicacy whatever, gives us a joint refusal in quite a loud voice.

"No, it will be better that you should be together. We have many visitors."

"Perhaps by tomorrow you may have two single rooms?"

"It is possible."

Later on, that phrase is to become familiar. It represents Soviet diplomacy. It means: "Your request is unheard of. It would be against the interests of the community to agree to it. Only a bourgeois mind could have thought of it. In no circumstances will any steps whatever be taken about it."

Tonight, Mrs. Pansy Baker and I are in equal

ignorance as to the meaning of the formula.
We do not fight against it, and both, I think,
try to look as though we *hadn't* protested so
earnestly at the idea of having to share a bedroom.

To be just, it is a large bedroom, and has a
modest little alcove with curtains, and an unsatisfactory and unhygienic little W. C. near the door,
where earwigs are active.

I suggest looking for a bathroom, but Mrs.
Pansy Baker says, less cheerfully than she usually
speaks, that she just can't share a bath-tub with
anybody. It may be very silly, but there it is. She
just can't do it.

I think I could take a very strong line here,
about the true Communistic spirit, but I don't and
only say that we should both probably be the better for some food.

We go down — the dining-room is large and
hideous and so, for that matter, are most of the
Comrades who are sitting in it—and have our first
meal on Russian soil.

It takes forty minutes to produce, fifteen minutes between each course, and about ten to eat.
The food is soup—very good—fish or meat—both

rather nasty—and ice-cream or compote. The ice-cream, says Mrs. Pansy Baker, is admirable. The compote is atrocious, composed of some unidentifiable fruit that is very hard and unripe, smothered in a quantity of thick syrup. When I find a little piece of tinned apricot lurking at the bottom I feel quite pleased and excited. It is like running into somebody from one's own Women's Institute, at the Annual General Meeting in London.

Mrs. Pansy Baker, unlike me, seems satisfied by what she has eaten, and tells me that tomorrow the tourists are to be taken for a drive round the town, and to be shown the Museum of the Revolution, a crèche for children, and the Isaac Cathedral. There may perhaps be time to do the Hermitage as well.

I ask if she is interested in pictures and she says No. As Professor Tod Mosher—the greatest of all English-speaking philosophers—puts it: This world is composed first and foremost, of thinking, feeling and living, *people*.

With this great thought to support us we go upstairs and unpack. I sprinkle Keatings on everything, like a pious acolyte scattering grains of incense, and we go to bed.

I VISIT THE SOVIETS

I daresay poor Mrs. Trollope's first night in America was a melancholy affair, except that she was no doubt thankful to get herself and all her children off the ship. A sea voyage in Mrs. Trollope's day and circumstances must have been a nightmare. . . .

I am pursuing large rats over the bodies of two prostrate little Trollopes when cries of excitement rouse me.

"I just had to wake you! This is one of the biggest moments of my life—this is what I crossed the Atlantic for, I guess!"

Surely, surely, Mrs. Pansy Baker didn't cross the Atlantic only in order to caper across the room in her dressing-gown and lean out of the window of the hotel?

"Listen!"

A ragged sound of distant voices reached me, and the tramp of a good many feet."

"Oh my, oh my, they're singing the 'Internationale' in the street!"

I am utterly indifferent to the "Internationale," which I didn't even recognize, but I am honestly impressed by Mrs. Pansy Baker and her enthusiasm.

Perhaps she really has more of Mrs. Trollope's spirit in her than I have?

(3)

In the morning, prepared for sight-seeing, we meet again with the Canadian engineer, the Armenian, and Miss Blake and Miss Bolton—besides an unknown German couple and an elderly Englishman who looks like H. G. Wells but, of course, isn't.

Whatever we may have felt about one another on the ship—and one really *must* remember that they probably viewed one very much in the same light that one viewed them—we now meet quite enthusiastically.

"Have you got a nice hotel?"

"Did you find your letters?"

"How is your flea?"

"Don't you think Leningrad is {
   wonderful?"
   dreary?"
   rather like
     Leeds?"

Miss Blake and Miss Bolton are amongst those

who think Leningrad dreary. They have been warped by finding cockroaches in their bedroom. Miss Bolton also tells me, aside, between closed teeth, that none of the plugs will pull. I feel superior and tell her that mine does but that there is no bedside lamp and I don't like the food, except the bread.

"Don't touch the black bread, it will give you diarrhoea."

We are full of sinister threats and warnings.

"Salad, I believe, is fatal. They grow it in drains."

"And I should be very doubtful of any fruit or any vegetables."

"Do tell me if your letters have been *opened*. I believe they censor everything."

"Did you notice a little ventilator in the bedroom? Of course it *might* be just nothing, but I suppose people *could* be listening through it."

We have got into a Gunpowder Plot atmosphere.

It is a good thing when the Canadian breaks in by enquiring why we were all told to be ready in the hall at 10 o'clock sharp, if we weren't going to start for three-quarters of an hour?

Nobody can tell him. Presently, when we have been longer in Russia, to be kept waiting will cease to be a matter for comment.

There is not a great deal to be seen, whilst we wait. The Intourist officials are nearly all women: they sit behind a long counter and write in ledgers, and telephone imperiously and give unsatisfactory replies to enquiries, just as people sitting behind counters always do, all over the world.

The elderly Englishman says, apparently to himself, that he hasn't yet seen a good-looking woman in Russia.

Neither have I. The feminine Comrades, so far, have displayed a disappointing similarity of appearance. They have bad figures, bad permanent waves, and very, very bad lipstick. Their faces are uninspiring. No doubt spies and countesses went out together, after the Revolution.

Not one of these drab, pallid, rather exhausted-looking women could be mistaken for either.

I am, I think, nearly as much disappointed as the elderly Englishman, and turn my attention to the notice on the wall.

A portrait of Lenin — bald, shrewd of eye and bearded — is flanked on either side by a gigantic poster. One of them displays Soviet Armenia—blossoming trees and young and lovely peasant girls in national head-dresses—the other one, The Georgian Highway: rocks and a huge bridge, all coloured blue, very unnaturally.

On the other side of the room is a board, with a list of theatres and cinemas in Russian. I find myself able to read this—it is not very difficult, as most of the plays are well-known ones and most of the films have already been heard of in England —and I gain a temporary fame by translating the titles to Miss Blake and Miss Bolton. I don't think they realize that I leave out all the words I can't understand.

All of a sudden a young woman with black hair and a worse lipstick than usual, rushes up to us.

"Please," she says imperiously.

She is our guide, and evidently feels that it is our fault, rather than hers, that the expedition is nearly an hour late in starting.

We are shepherded into a motor-bus and rattled round the town, over an atrocious surface, neglected for years.

That is, in fact, one's main impression of Leningrad: it has been neglected for years.

The tall, beautiful Empire buildings are slowly disintegrating as they stand.

"What are those lovely houses in that Crescent?"

"They were the homes of the rich aristocracy."

"What are they now?"

"They will be taken down, and modern dwellings constructed for the workers. Some of them are now clubs for the workers. In the Revolution of 1905——"

The guide is off.

The Revolution of 1905, the Revolution of 1917. She speaks of them continually, and always with the same enthusiasm. Her capacity for Soviet propaganda is unlimited.

She takes us to see a clinic for children whose mothers are working in a nearby factory.

The children are out of doors, playing in a courtyard, there are two women in charge, there are little cots in which they can take a midday sleep, and little mugs and toothbrushes hanging on pegs round the dormitory, with a picture of Comrade Stalin—bristling black hair and moustache and very much the air of a *bon bourgeois* en-

dimanché—surmounting the toothbrushes.

All—except possibly Stalin, whom I should prefer to see replaced by Mother Goose or Cinderella—is admirable.

It is not, however, nearly as clean or as well-equipped as any similar institutions in England or in America would be—nor do the children look as healthy, and the fact that all their little heads are shorn and they are wearing striped overalls gives them a queer resemblance to infant convicts.

I should be more enthusiastic if Mrs. Pansy Baker and the Guide were less so.

"In Soviet Russia all the women have the right to work, they work the same like a man. They leave here their children, five hours, eight hours, twelve hours."

"What about Sundays?" says the elderly Englishman.

He has made a fearful error, and all of us know it and gaze at him appalled. The Guide seems to stiffen all over.

"We have not here the days of the week. Every sixth day is a rest day. But there are no Sundays, Mondays. We have not."

A momentary silence envelopes us all, and the

ghosts of the Sundays and Mondays of capitalist countries seem to slink past into an unhonoured Limbo.

The Guide is the first to rally.

She tells us about women-workers, about pregnant women, nursing mothers, women who wish to undergo an operation for abortion, and women at the period of menstruation.

How extraordinarily outspoken she is.

The Canadian stands up to it well, and even puts in an intelligent question or two. So do the Germans. The elderly Englishman walks away, and pats the heads of some of the infant convicts, who thereupon dribble.

Miss Blake, Miss Bolton and I merely listen and say nothing.

Mrs. Pansy Baker ejaculates and admires and declares that everything is wonderful.

As for the Armenian, who has never uttered at all, he continues to be silent and to smoke cigarettes. I don't think he is interested.

"In capitalist countries you have not such help for the mothers, no?" enquires the guide.

"I should say not!" cries Mrs. Pansy Baker—just as the Canadian says:

"Why, sure we have!"

"No, you have not," says the guide. "It is only in the Soviet State."

It turns out later that this is her attitude throughout. In Soviet Russia everything is good: elsewhere everything is bad.

She is, I suppose, about thirty years old and has never been out of Russia. Her English, which is very fluent, has been acquired in a Technical School in Moscow.

She has an answer to every single question. Usually it is an answer that extols the U.S.S.R. When this is impossible she simply says:

"It is being arranged by the Government."

As none of us are in a position to contradict her, she always gets the last word.

At 3 o'clock we return to the hotel for lunch, at 4 o'clock we get it. Soup, good — fish, very nasty—ice-cream excellent and a good alternative to the compote. Not, however, substantial. I am still hungry.

If I eat the bread I shall get diarrhoea. Everybody says so.

Mrs. Trollope, we know, was very often in no position to get any food at all, for herself or her children.

Perhaps, however, she found it less expensive and difficult than I do to get ordinary cold water to drink. Only the Russian mineral water, which is very dear, is good. Tea in a glass, with or without lemon, needs getting used to — but I shall do it.

I must think of Mrs. Trollope.

Especially when I get my first letters from home.

(4)

"The Winter Palace of the Tsars, now the Museum of the Revolution."

The guide here is in her element. The Revolutions of 1905 and 1917, as well as earlier and more abortive ones, are featured on a grand scale.

It is an orgy of propaganda.

Large and crude paintings hang on all the walls —peasants shooting, soldiers shooting, peasants being shot, revolutionaries plotting in cellars, the *bourgeoisie* drinking beer and the aristocracy drinking champagne—and on every wall, Lenin.

There are little alcoves, with waxwork groups

[105]

featuring very much the same kind of thing, and there are reproductions of peasant hovels and bourgeois mansions.

Historical value exists only in the photographs that are contemporary with the events they depict, and in some of the documents, framed and hanging against the walls.

The rest is violent propaganda of a kind that can only appeal to an unsophisticated and uneducated mentality.

During most of the tour, which lasts nearly three hours, I occupy myself in trying to visualize the Winter Palace as it must have looked in the old, bad, Imperial days.

Finally the guide shows us a photograph of the very room in which we are standing, taken just after the mob broke into the palace in 1917.

The glass of the windows is all splintered by bullets, the Empire furniture is standing on its head, or lying in fragments.

It is, I suppose, a very typical minor result of revolution; a mob, swayed by mob-emotion, driven mad by past wrongs and present licence and venting its excitement in acts of destruction.

I have no comment to make on the photograph,

but Mrs. Pansy Baker has.

"It's just grand," she says emotionally, "to think of all those splendid workers forcing their way in, and destroying all this wicked luxury. I just wish I had been with them!"

For the moment I too wish she had, and had seen and heard and felt what it was really like. . . .

This, I think, is the time for saying that Mrs. Pansy Baker is *not* a typical American, and that one has never thought her so. Most of the Americans met by the new Mrs. Trollope in Russia were charming, intelligent and kind. Indeed, Mrs. Pansy Baker herself is not without charm, kindness and intelligence. She is always vital and alert, always interested, and not wholly without humour.

She is only quite devoid of imagination, of a sense of proportion and of the capacity for seeing any point of view but the one that she has swallowed wholesale from Professor Tod Mosher. Now that I come to think of it, the U.S.S.R. is exactly the right place for her.

She had better settle here.

I don't believe Mr. Baker and the two children would mind.

And the excellence of this idea is confirmed,

once and for all, when I myself—from sheer curiosity—ask Mrs. Pansy Baker a question.

"Granted that the Revolution had to come, and that the country is the better for it, do you ever feel that it was rather dreadful to have to shed so much blood in order to bring it about?"

She shakes her head.

"I don't look at it that way. It was necessary."

"Do you know the story of the murder of the Imperial family?"

"I guess they were just shot."

"Yes, all of them. Shot down in a cellar, the Emperor and Empress, and five children, of whom the youngest was an invalid boy. And the members of the household who went with them into exile. They were all shot too. All massacred together, in the cellar."

"Was that so?" ejaculates Mrs. Pansy Baker thoughtfully. She is silent for a moment and then, with an agreeable smile, sums up the whole thing.

"I guess," she remarks tolerantly, "that it was done as kindly as possible."

THEY ALSO SERVE

THERE IS NO UNEMPLOYMENT IN THE
Soviet Union: everybody can, and indeed must,
work—and so far as I know everybody does. As a
kind of offset to this universal activity everybody
—when not working—sits about and waits.

At the Leningrad Hotel I, also, sit about and
wait. I wait for the Intourist Bureau to telephone
to the people to whom I have brought letters of
introduction. I wait for the lift, which has just
taken three Comrades upstairs, to come down
again — which it never does. I wait for my 10
o'clock supper—ordered at 9, and brought—with
any luck—at about 11. I sit in the hall and wait,
for nothing in particular. I am becoming Russianized.

A very old man comes in, wearing a fur cap and
a coat. (*Ancien régime*, like a picture in an old
nursery-book.) He sits down on a fraction of a
bench which is already occupied by two French
ladies, a girl in a blouse and skirt, and a Comrade
smoking a cigarette.

There are never enough seats to go round, in
the hotel. Most of the people who come in and

[109]

wait have to wait on their feet, leaning against walls. They do it fatalistically, obviously inured. The enormous shabby portfolios they all carry—like degraded music-cases—lie at their feet.

What, I wonder, are all these cases? They can't *all* be carrying important secret documents for the Government. Yet all the Comrades have portfolios, except the very old man who has a newspaper parcel instead, from which protrudes the tail of a fish. Perhaps the Comrades who are less *ancien régime* carry their fish in portfolios? The old man, I am sorry to say, spits.

I turn my attention elsewhere.

An English tourist has come into the bureau, and I know by the brisk and business-like way in which he begins that he is newly-arrived, and has no experience of Russian methods — unlike me. (At this I feel elderly and superior, and think of Julia Mills and the Desert of Sahara.)

"There's a man I want to get hold of as soon as possible," says the Englishman blithely. "I haven't got his address, but you'll find him in the telephone-book. Harrison, the name is."

"Harrison?"

"Harrison."

"You do not know where he lives?"

"I'm afraid not."

"Not in which street is his apartment?"

"No. But he'll be in the telephone-book."

"Perhaps you know where is his office?"

"No, but——"

"Not in which street is his office?"

"I only know that his name is Harrison, and he's in Leningrad, and you'll find him in the telephone-book."

"Ah. But you have not his address."

"It'll be in the telephone-book."

"Ah."

There is a long silence. At this stage — for I have heard this dialogue before, and have often taken part in it myself — some English tourists, and most American ones, look round for the telephone-book and swoop down upon it. This Englishman, however, is of inferior mettle. Or perhaps he has Russian blood in him.

He waits.

Presently Intourist utters once more.

"He has a telephone number?"

"Yes. He'll be in the book."

"Ah. It is at his house, or at his office, the telephone?"

"His office, I think."

"And the name it is *Harrison?*"

"Harrison."

Faint demonstrations of searching for the book.

"The book it is not here. I will send."

A young blonde, who has, to my certain knowledge, been standing waiting for the better part of an hour, is sent to fetch the book. Perhaps it is for that and nothing else that she has been waiting? Intourist waits, the Englishman waits, we all wait.

The French ladies on the bench have begun to mutter to one another, low and venomously.

"Mais voilà—elle n'a pas de cœur. Tout simplement. Elle manque de cœur."

"Ça, par exemple—NON!"

"Moi, je vous dis que si."

"Moi, je vous dis que non."

Deadlock.

The very old man has now, I think, fallen into a coma. What an abominable thing it is to keep him waiting all this time! He is a hard-working peasant, and his haughty employer, the Grand Duke, is upstairs drinking champagne—

I VISIT THE SOVIETS

What am I thinking of? The poor Grand Duke is, if fortunate, giving dancing lessons somewhere on the Riviera. The old man is a worker, a Comrade—he is quite all right.

Still, I don't think they need keep him waiting such a very long while.

Presently the blonde returns with the telephonebook, and Intourist begins to turn over the leaves, and to say once more:

"Harrison?"

"Harrison."

"Ah, Harrison." A long pause.

"No. He is not here."

"But I think he *must* be. I say, would you mind if I had a look?"

The Englishman has a look, and runs Harrison to ground in a moment.

"Here he is! A. M. Harrison—that's the man."

"Ah? He is in the book?"

Intourist is only mildly surprised, and not in the least interested. The blonde, in a thoughtful way, says into space:

"Harrison."

The voices of the French ladies surge upwards once more.

"Ah! son mari! Comme je le plains!"

"Et moi, non. Au contraire."

I should like to know more of the ménage under discussion—they can't *both* be right—but they shrug their shoulders simultaneously, glare, and say nothing more.

The Harrison quest goes on. I say to myself: We are progressing slowly, ma'am. If I knew as many quotations from Shakespeare, or Plato, or even Karl Marx, as I do from Dickens, I should hold a very different, and much more splendid, place in the ranks of the literary.

"You want that I should telephone to him, yes?"

"Please. If you will."

Intourist will.

But not at once.

"It is his apartment, or his office?"

"Well, I don't really know—but whichever number is in the book will find him, I expect."

"I will try," says Intourist pessimistically.

They know, and I know, that their pessimism is justified. The Englishman, as yet, does not know.

He waits—I suppose hopefully — and the telephone is brought into action.

[114]

I VISIT THE SOVIETS

It is customary—necessary, for all I know to the contrary—to shriek, rather than speak into it, and the first fifteen 'Allos meet with no acknowledgment. Then something happens. The Exchange has replied.

The two French ladies, tired of looking angrily at one another, turn their heads—the blonde lifts hers from its apathetic angle—only the old man is unmoved. (Disgraceful, that he should have been ignored so long. I believe no one has so much as asked him what he wants. Hotel servants the same all the world over, Comrades or no Comrades.)

"Shall I——?" says the Englishman, ready to leap at the receiver.

"The number is bee-zy."

"Busy?"

"It is bee-zy. If you will wait a little, I will try once more."

We all settle down again.

A woman with a baby—and a portfolio—comes into the hotel with a business-like air, and goes up and speaks to the porter in Russian.

He nods.

Like Jove, I think—and ought to be pleased to

find that I am moving a step away from Dickens and towards the classics—but on the other hand I like Dickens, and I don't even know the classics.

The woman with the baby sits down, in the absence of any unoccupied chair, on a marble step leading to the barber's shop, and waits.

I wonder what amount of information Jove can have conveyed to her in that single nod for her to know—as she presumably does—that it is going to be worth her while to sit down and wait.

Presently the French ladies get up. They both say "Eh bien!" and the one who *didn't* pity the husband adds "A quelque chose, malheur est bon" in a philosophical way.

They move towards the lift, their mysterious allusions for ever unexplained.

Not that they leave us immediately. Far from it. They have to wait for the lift. Then they have to wait because the lift can only take four people, and there are already three inside it and they decline—fiercely—to go separately.

"Mais passez donc——"

"Non, non, non. Allez, je vous en prie."

"Mais non, mais non. Allez, vous——"

I VISIT THE SOVIETS

"Du tout."

A solitary Ukranian who has been waiting—probably for the lift—for hours, is encouraged by the liftman to take advantage of this indecision and fill the vacant place.

He does so and the French ladies are left, shrugging their shoulders again. One of them says that it is "fantastique."

The bench on which the old man of the *ancien régime* is sitting has now two vacant places, which are at once filled by four people. They take advantage of the old man's state of suspended animation to shove him and his fish to the extremest edge of the seat. I think that presently he will fall off.

The Englishman is still seeking his Harrison.

"I should think you might give them another ring, now."

"I will try."

The effort is made.

"There is no reply from that number."

"No reply?"

"No. I think it is his office. It does not answer."

"But there must be somebody there."

"There is nobody there. Today it is the day of rest. The offices are all shut."

I VISIT THE SOVIETS

The Englishman is staggered. I can positively see the thoughts flying through his mind.

Tuesday, the day of rest? By Jove, yes! there are no Sundays in Russia now, but they have a holiday every sixth day. Then why on earth couldn't they say so sooner? Of course the offices *would* be shut. Good God, what a country!

"I suppose I'd better try again tomorrow morning," he says angrily. "Unless you could ask the Exchange if they know the number of his private house?"

"You want to ask the telephone number of his house?"

"If they can give it to you."

"Ah. I can ask them, if you wish."

He does wish.

A little boy with a shaven head and bare feet and carrying a small attaché-case, comes in and adds to the congestion on the bench.

The lift returns and the two French ladies, after a few passes as to which of them shall enter it first, get inside. Then they wait again while the liftman looks for a singleton passenger. He may not take more than four people at a time, but is determined not to take less.

I VISIT THE SOVIETS

The Englishman is now leaning against the wall with his arms folded. Russia is growing on him. I can see it plainly.

"They ring his apartment," says Intourist. "They say there is no reply."

"He must be away."

"He is bee-zy. Or perhaps he is seek."

These are the favourite alternatives of Intourist, when a telephone connection is unobtainable. They do not say that the number is engaged, or the telephone out of order. They make the less impersonal suggestion that the owner of the required number is either busy—too busy, presumably, to answer his telephone calls   or that he is ill.

The Englishman says that he supposes he must wait till to-morrow. Already, he seems to me to be wilting slightly.

As he moves away from the Intourist Bureau he stops and reads a notice informing him that Excursions will start punctually at 10 o'clock each morning and tourists must on no account be late. I wonder if he believes it?

Perhaps I have been here long enough, and ought to give up my chair to one of the numerous Comrades who are standing about doing nothing.

I am not really waiting for anything in particular—
only just waiting. But I should like to see somebody
pay a little attention to the ancient in the fur cap.
He has been waiting longer than anybody else, and
has probably got rooted to his minute fragment of
the bench, by this time.

Comrades come and Comrades go, the blonde
in the office folds her arms on a table and lays her
head upon them, the Englishman buys a copy of
the *Moscow Daily News* and reads about Abortion
—at least I suppose he does, as the papers devote
much more space to that than to any other subject
—and the Comrade with the cigarette gets up and
is followed by the Comrade in the blouse and skirt,
who has been sitting next him all the time but with
whom he has never exchanged word or look. But
they go away arm-in-arm and are, no doubt, husband and wife in the sight of Stalin.

Other people drift in, and take their places, and
wait. The old man comes out of his coma. He is
going to demand attention. To insist upon doing
whatever it is that he has come to do and for which
he has waited so interminably.

Not at all.

He picks up his fish, rises very slowly to his feet,

and walks out again into the street. He came, apparently, for the express purpose of sitting and waiting, and for nothing else.

How little he knows that he has supplied me with the title for this article.

MARGARET WAS RIGHT

WE LIVE AND MOVE IN GROUPS. IN-
tourist, referring to the English Group, means anybody who speaks English. There is a German
Group, which often includes Dutch and Swedish
and Finnish tourists. The French Group, when it
exists at all, is usually composed exclusively of
French people. In Leningrad a miscellaneous
Group, of which I am one, is taken by auto-bus to
visit the two Palaces at Tsarskoe Selo: one of them
the Palace of Catherine II, incredibly large and
glittering and with inlaid floors and amber walls
and lapis lazuli columns—so that when I get there
I think of Aladdin and look for the roc's egg—and
the other one the Alexander Palace, where the last
Tsar and Tsarina lived with their children during
the last year of their lives.

Mrs. Pansy Baker is with us, indomitable as
ever, although to my certain knowledge she was
up half the night and didn't get her supper till
1 A.M. She has annexed a Russian who can speak
no word of English but who believes that if he
says things often enough in Russian we shall all
understand them. Mrs. Pansy Baker is equally con-

[122]

vinced that with a very little effort on his part, and a raised voice on hers, he will surely take in the meaning of everything that she says to him in English.

When this fails she looks humorously round at the rest of us and says:

"Oh my, oh my! I don't believe he's following me. Did you ever? I guess you don't understand me, do you? Isn't that too bad?"

The Canadian engineer is with us. He speaks little, but from time to time morosely contradicts Mrs. Pansy Baker when she makes inaccurate assertions about Communism. For this we are all grateful to him.

(Mrs. Pansy Baker says she is, too, but I don't believe it.)

A Swedish gentleman is with us. He tells us that he is a pedagogue. It turns out eventually that he is a school inspector. He is energetic, and springs about a good deal, and talks several languages very fluently and loudly, and he wears a long blue cape that swings round him in a dramatic kind of way, and a little blue béret crammed onto the back of his head.

He is sitting between Miss Blake and Miss Bolton, and I think they don't like the separation.

They keep on looking at one another across him, and sometimes they speak—to one another, not to him.

"Did you remember about the Lux, Bolton?"

"Yes. I did the Lux."

"I hope the things won't *drip*."

"I don't think so."

On second thoughts, though, Miss Bolton evidently does think so. After looking fearfully worried for some ten or fifteen seconds she leans forward again.

"It isn't as though it was a carpet, after all."

"No. Wouldn't you like my scarf?"

"No, no. I'm not cold."

"You'd be more comfortable if you had it, I think."

"No, really."

"I don't want it. You'd better have it."

The Swedish pedagogue, who has swung himself round as if he were on a swivel to face each speaker in turn, cries to Miss Bolton in a loud, cheerful voice:

"You are cold, yes?"

"No thank you, I'm not cold at all."

"But you want the scarf, no?"

"It's all right, thank you."

"It's quite all right, thank you," Miss Blake supports her. But I notice she gives her a reproachful look all the same. I suppose about the scarf.

The car shoots round a corner—there are very few cars in Leningrad, and this is as well, for the Comrades drive with great *insouciance*—and the guide points out a building and says, "The British Embassy at the time of the Revolution."

Like nearly all the buildings in Leningrad, it looks unspeakably neglected and in need of paint. Mrs. Pansy Baker says My! it's too bad, to think of a great palace like that housing just one man, and then adds winningly that she maybe oughtn't to have said that, but anyway we're all friends here —at which most of us exchange glances of loathing and contempt.

"At that window," says the guide, pointing to a little iron balcony, "Sir Buchanan, the British Ambassador, spoke to the workers of the October Revolution."

I ask what he said.

"I do not know."

The guide is young and tiresome. (She probably thinks all of us old and tiresome. She may even—

unpleasant and quite unexpected thought—have some grounds for thinking so.)

Sir Buchanan is left behind. In much brisker tones the guide points out the Museum of the Revolution—which I saw yesterday and disliked, —and the Red Square—and the Isaac Cathedral, now an Anti-religion Museum. I realize—not for the first time—that this is no country for me and that I can't imagine why I ever came to it.

"In this street were the palaces of the aristocracy, now converted into apartment-houses for the workers."

And what, I think, has happened to the aristocracy? But this is the wrong reaction. Everybody else is saying how splendid it all is, and admiring the apartment-houses. Curious that nobody has, apparently, thought of giving them a coat of paint.

As usual, innumerable Comrades are walking about the streets and thronging the rusty, dilapidated-looking trams that totter and shake along their way. "You see, the people are all busy. They walk. They are not *aimless*," says the guide. I think of replying that perhaps their aim is to get out of Leningrad?—but do not do so. I fancy that very few jokes are really successful in the Soviet Union, and that the jokes of foreigners would stand a particularly poor chance.

Besides, Mrs. Pansy Baker is speaking. She says it's perfectly wonderful.

("Do have my scarf, Bolton."

"Honestly, I don't want it. But don't you want it yourself? Why not put it on?"

"Oh, I'm not cold. But I wish you'd have it.")

"Yes," says the guide, "it is wonderful. It is wonderful to see so many people happy, and with work to do. On the right, the Park of Rest and Culture."

We all look reverently at the Park of Rest and Culture, where a number of exhausted-looking old women are jostling one another on benches, and small children are screaming and falling about, and a loud-speaker is blaring, and an enormous poster of Comrade Stalin, with his hair *en brosse*, is smiling rather ferociously down on the crowd from the kiosk at the gate.

"On the left, new apartment-houses."

The new apartment-houses have balconies. They look clean and pleasant, and I should like to know how many rooms are allotted to each family.

The guide becomes evasive, when I put the ques-

[127]

tion. "We have still a housing problem. In some cases they have more rooms, in some less," she answers—leaving me where she found me, which is what she doubtless intended.

"Those balconies are just as cute!" cries Mrs. Pansy Baker. Quite as though she'd never seen a balcony on any apartment-house in the whole of the United States in her life.

The Russian says something in Russian.

"I guess he's telling me that in ten years' time they'll have put up a whole lot more of the same kind, with bath-tubs and elevators for each family."

"No," says the Canadian—evidently on principle, since he knows not a word of Russian. "No, he's not."

The auto-bus whisks us out into a long country road, stacked with drain-pipes, choked with lorries, crawling with workers.

"Construction-work," says the guide.

The construction-work lands us in and out of pot-holes, jolts us into ruts and out of them, and several times threatens to overturn us altogether.

"Disgraceful!" exclaims the pedagogue, suddenly and strongly. And he tells us about roads in Sweden, which are all quite different.

The Park of Rest and Culture.

I VISIT THE SOVIETS

"What are they constructing?" enquires the Canadian engineer.

"Apartment-houses for the workers."

"Won't they be a long way from their work?"

"No. They will build factories here."

How well-trained these guides are. They have answers for everything. They are like Parliamentary candidates. Perhaps they are provided with a kind of little Catechism, giving (probable) questions and (desirable) answers. I should like to think of some startlingly original question, to see if it would baffle them.

"This is the beginning of Tsarskoe Selo. It is now a Children's Home."

"Isn't that just too lovely!"

It is my absolute conviction that if the Soviet Government were to turn the Kremlin into a Home for Crocodiles Mrs. Pansy Baker would ask if that wasn't just too lovely.

There are queer, picturesque little wooden shacks along the side of the road, each with a red rag loyally waving from it.

"Some of the old dwellings," says the guide, looking at them witheringly, "They will be pulled down soon."

I quite see that she's right. I quite see that they must go. But they've been homes for a long time, and they look pretty, and surely they can't be much more uncomfortable than the new apartment-houses where not more than one room, or two at most, can be spared for a whole family? I know that this is a thoroughly sentimental way of looking at the whole thing, and that I must make an effort, like Mrs. Dombey. I am inspired to tell myself, in a whisper, to Rouge yourself Mr. Chuffey — and unfortunately Miss Bolton overhears me and says "Pardon?" in a startled way.

"Nothing. I didn't say anything."

"If you're cold, Miss Blake has a scarf that she isn't wearing."

"Yes, I know she has. But I'm not cold, thank you."

"It is not cold!" cries the Swedish pedagogue, and he throws out his chest, and flings back his cloak—(Miss Blake's eye in great danger of being put out)—and snuffs up the air through his nose, like a horse.

We all instinctively draw ourselves up too, and try to look equally martial—and a very poor job most of us make of it. And the guide smiles, and shakes her head, and remarks in a very superior and knowledgeable way: No, it is not cold. She means, I think, that it is only in Capitalist countries that people can have any cause to complain about the weather.

Presently we turn into a little avenue, and into a courtyard, and the auto-bus stops and we all get out.

The Palace of Catherine II is before us, and before the Palace are vast numbers of Comrades, all disporting themselves, just like a Blackpool holiday crowd.

They are not behaving badly: they have every right to be here, it all belongs to them, now. They are harmlessly enjoying themselves in the open air, playing on instruments, and sprawling about, and spitting, and walking up and down in rows with linked arms. Theoretically, I feel sure they ought to be there.

Actually, I am seized with dismay and can only think of all the wrong things: the dispossessed nobility, the genius that built the Palace and laid out the grounds with quite other ends in view, the country hush that is shattered by the proletarian revellings.

And quite suddenly I remember that before I left England, Margaret, thoughtfully and without malice, remarked to me that she had always thought I was a snob.

Now why should that come into my head just now? At the time I merely thought—as one always does when people say that kind of thing—that she didn't really mean it. (Why? If she had said that I was the most charming woman of her acquaintance I shouldn't have known the least qualm of doubt as to whether she really meant it. I should have taken it for granted that she did.) I wish I hadn't remembered it just now.

The Palace is enormous, and a great deal of it is in *baroque* style, with much heavy gilt moulding and bright blue paint. Full and admirable descriptions of it are to be found in the guide-books, where I hope that justice is also done to those reception-rooms that are beautiful, and like the Arabian Nights. The walls of one are faced with amber, of another with mother-o'-pearl, of another with lapis-lazuli. There are chairs, covered in exquisite petit-point, against the walls—and lovely paintings—and Chinese panellings.

If only there was no guide, and no group, and

no large parties of shuffling and muttering sight-seers just ahead and just behind, how much more I should enjoy it all. I know it's not right, but that's how I feel.

The Swedish gentleman is roaring apprecia-tively, and asking intelligent questions as to where the amber came from, and how long it took to in-lay the floor, and Mrs. Pansy Baker is shaking her head in disapproval of it all, and Miss Blake and Miss Bolton are talking in undertones, and I hear the word "vest" pass between them several times, and once Miss Bolton says that something —I can't catch what—"isn't like a gas-ring." I dare say not.

We see the ballroom—or perhaps it's a banquet-ing-hall—and it has a special echo, and the guide goes into the middle of the room and addresses it in a ringing voice, so that it replies. And I captiously reflect how much better it must have sounded when it echoed to strains of music, in-stead of to the inanities of a young woman with a shrill voice and an uneducated intonation.

Naturally, I keep this thought to myself—and am, in fact, slightly ashamed of it and again, un-willingly, remember Margaret.

Then we are taken outside again.

The Alexander Palace is what I have really come to see, although I haven't said so. Amongst all the many books that I ought to have read, and haven't read, before coming to Russia, there are exceptions. I have read the story of the last days of the Romanovs.

We pass amongst some trees, and there is — comparatively speaking—quite a *little* palace. No larger than some of England's big country-houses. Near the front of it is a narrow strip of garden and growing in a bed, violas—the first flowers, I think, that I have seen in Russia.

"Pansies—that's for remembrance."

But I don't say this aloud, and nobody hears it.

Then we pass inside, and the guide becomes talkative and efficient, and Mrs. Pansy Baker ejaculatory.

The Swede is striding along and has grasped Miss Blake by the arm—I think quite impersonally—and is telling her something about the children of Sweden.

The Russian is stalking, solitary, behind Miss Bolton, and Miss Bolton is hunting madly inside her bag for something that won't be found.

I VISIT THE SOVIETS

For a second, the eyes of the Canadian meet mine, and I think I see in them the grave reflection of my own feelings.

"Now we are in the private rooms of the family. Here, they sat in the evenings. You will see in how very bad taste are the rooms. It was all in that style, what they had. All in very bad taste. Even the pictures they are bad."

Are they? There are a very great number of them, and there are quantities and quantities of signed photographs. All the relations of the Tsarina, German and English, and a painting of old Queen Victoria, and signed photographs. . . . Memories of far-away countries and of days long gone by.

"There are many, many portraits of her—of the Tsarina—she was painted very often. She was very vain," says the guide complacently, in the tone of one who knows. She is, perhaps, somewhere in her middle twenties, and to her the Romanovs are not real people at all. They are only part of the glorious history of the Revolution. She has been told what to say about them, and she says it, and doubts not at all but that the whole of the truth is contained in her little glib parrot-phrases.

There are, as she says, many portraits of the Tsarina. In some of the early ones she looks almost gay — young and pretty, and very like a du Maurier drawing. Quite early, she must have grown grave and very serious, and always with a faint look of anxiety across these level dark brows. None of the later pictures are smiling ones, not even when she is portrayed with the four little dark-haired girls close beside her. And not when her small, frail only son lies in her arms.

One picture of her, in court robes, hangs in her husband's library high up on the wall. It shows the sad, obtuse, beautiful face under a diamond crown.

There are pictures of the Tsar too.

He is very like our own King George V.

"The Tsar's room, where he received his ministers. There is a secret staircase, leading to the room of the Tsarina, so that she could listen——"

And I look at the photographs, and close my ears.

There are books in the room too—a great many of them, in glass-fronted bookshelves. Most of them are beautifully bound—and then comes a row of Tauchnitz novels, all English. And a copy of *Tartarin sur les Alpes*, and I wonder if the Grand Duchesses read it in the schoolroom, and laughed.

"This was the bedroom of the Tsarina. You see, it was quite a little room, and so crowded, and all in such bad taste. And all the ikons—she was very superstitious, she would pray for hours . . ."

Yes, it is quite a little room. The bed and the dressing-table and the *bergère* still have their faded pink draperies. Religious emblems cover the walls —there are crucifixes, and ikons, and pictures of the Virgin and Child.

She prayed for hours.

There are photographs, and more photographs. All the children — the pretty, long-haired girls in plain white muslin frocks with high necks, and a photograph, on a little table all by itself, of the Tsar in naval uniform.

It is signed "Nicky."

"It has all been kept just as she left it. See, here are her things——"

The things are in a little glass-topped table. An ivory étui, and a small gold thimble, and some embroidery scissors. All kinds of odds and ends, and all rather worn and used. There are even one or two cheap toys—a china bird and a pincushion made like a shoe. The kind of things that one of the children might have given her.

"They are not even preet-ty," says the guide contemptuously.

She has no remotest conception that "prettiness"—by which she means in fashion—is a relative term, dependent on time and place, and that twenty-five years hence the standards of today will have given place to others, just as those of today have replaced those of twenty-five years ago.

She moves on into the adjoining room with her group and I can still hear her shrill, uninflected voice.

"The bedroom of the Tsar. The taste is very bad —the lamp-shade that terrible colour——"

And in the room of the Tsarina, where I linger, an elderly caretaker comes in by another door, on the far side of the rope that divides the room from the tourists.

She is going to dust all the things—what a lot of dusting they must need, there are so many of them!—but first, she looks at me and I look at her.

Neither of us speaks the other's language, and we exchange not a word. Only that look.

She picks up from the table by the bedside a photograph in a leather frame and carries it across to where I stand, and holds it out for me to see; and it is the Tsarevitch—a dark-haired, dark-eyed, serious little boy in an English sailor-suit.

"We go now upstairs, to see the children's rooms. They are only on the next floor."

I tell the guide that I will wait downstairs. I don't wish to come up to the second floor.

"You are not interested?"

"I would rather sit down here and wait for you."

"No, please. You will come. The rooms are very inter-esting. They are just as they left them when they went away."

The guide, perhaps naturally, does not wish the members of her group to be separated. She becomes anxious, and rather insistent, till I say that I will sit on a bench in the garden and remain there without moving till they all come back again.

Then she reluctantly leaves me. Just as she is turning to go, a bright idea for my entertainment appears to strike her, and she turns back again.

"That window—you can see from where you are —it is through there that they went away. They were not allowed to go by the front door, the carriage it came to the side door. It was through there that they went away, on the last day, for their last drive."

"On their way to Ekaterinburg?"

"On their way to Ekaterinburg," she agrees cheerfully.

She lingers a moment longer to offer me a further inducement to accompany the group upstairs.

"I can show you even the toys of the children, that they left behind."

But I shake my head, and stay where I am, in view of the glass door through which the Romanovs were taken away, down the road that led in the end to the cellar of the House of Ipatievsky.

When the group is shepherded downstairs again, only Mrs. Pansy Baker and the Swedish pedagogue are still talking.

The others are silent.

"You didn't come upstairs?" says Miss Bolton, eyeing me rather curiously.

"No."

"They showed us everything. Even the toys that the Imperial children—"

"Yes, I know."

Miss Blake, in a low voice, says:

"There was a motor-car that had belonged to the little boy. It was his favourite toy."

And we all fall silent again.

"There is no more," says the guide merrily. "We have seen all."

Once more we pass the Comrades, thronging the courtyard. Very likely they are quite different Comrades, but they all look and sound to me exactly like the ones we saw when we arrived.

"My, just look at that fellow! Isn't he cute, with that accordion thing of his? I guess he's just as musical as ever he can be!" carols Mrs. Pansy Baker.

"No he isn't."

I hope with all my heart that the Canadian's answer, which in its promptness amounts almost to violence, is as great a relief to his feelings as it is to mine.

I think, somehow, that it is.

On the way back, a great deal of talk passes between the pedagogue and Mrs. Pansy Baker, about Communism. Miss Blake and Miss Bolton make many efforts to join in, but they are not loud enough, or fluent enough. I gather that they are not Communists, because they begin their sentences with "Yes, but look here, *if*——" and the rest, if there is any, is lost.

They are obliged to fall back upon the gas-ring, metaphorically speaking, and by the end of the drive it has taken them all the way to a hand-knitted jumper bought at a Summer Sale two years ago by someone whom Miss Blake refers to as "me friend."

(I don't think she ought to say "me friend," as if that was the only one she had. Miss Bolton's feelings will be hurt. She should say "one of me friends" or even "me other friend.")

The Swede is springing up and down in his seat, quoting Karl Marx.

Mrs. Pansy Baker approves Karl Marx, asserting that what he says is *Right*.

"You have read all his works, yes?" enquires the guide.

If that question had been put by the Canadian engineer—or, for that matter, by me—it would have had a totally different tang about it. The guide asks it trustfully and innocently, and—to do Mrs. Pansy Baker justice—gets a moderately truthful reply.

"Well, no, I can't say I've read all of them. I am a very much occupied woman, and much as I would like to devote my entire time to sociological research, I just can't do it. The claims upon me are very numerous, and very varied. Mr. Baker is not as much in sympathy with my work as I could wish, and I am forced to sacrifice a certain amount of time to satisfying his requirements at home."

(Mrs. Jellaby.)

"And I have three very lovely children, besides."

(Caddy Jellaby, and poor little Peepy?)

"I take the claims of motherhood very seriously," says Mrs. Pansy Baker, giving me a glance. I know already, since she has told me so, that she feels the claims of motherhood, in my case, have been a good deal overlooked. Otherwise what am I, who am not even politically minded, doing all by myself in Soviet Russia?

She little knows how often I ask myself the same question.

"In the United States of America, the education of the children is largely based on a psychological——"

She has made a fatal error.

The pedagogue knows his own subject when he

hears it mentioned, and will yield it to no living man or woman.

He roars — quite pleasantly and fluently — all the rest of the way.

Miss Blake and Miss Bolton fall quite silent, the Canadian gazes out at the buildings of Leningrad —which is, after all, one of the objects of the expedition—Mrs. Pansy Baker looks very intelligent and nods a great deal and tries to interrupt, but doesn't get a look in—and the guide and the Russian gentleman exchange sentences in Russian. I can make out the words "Lenin," "worker," "Soviet" and "capitalism" which recur again and again.

How thoroughgoing they are! Do they *never* think or speak about anything but the constitution of their country? Still, it covers a wide field. I find myself making up an alphabet of Russian conversational topics.

A for Abortion, or Abolition—of Nobility, Religion, Capitalism, Prostitutes, etc.

B for Bortsch, and Birth -control.

C for Comrades or Construction, or Constitution.

D for Demolition—Democracy—

and so on. I shall enjoy doing S, which is particularly fruitful, with Stalin, Stakanovite, Soviet System, Socialism and probably a great many more. Perhaps when it is all finished I shall send it up to *Pravda* and they will print it as an English witticism?

"You are sleepy, no?" says the guide to me, kindly.

"Perhaps I am."

"Oh my, oh my! I just can't fancy anybody wanting to sleep here. It's all so *stimulating.*"

Mrs. Pansy Baker turns to the Russian—perhaps hoping that he has thought things over in the interval since she last spoke to him and has at last made up his mind to understand English.

"This English Comrade and I have been put in the same bedroom to sleep, in the hotel, and I guess she can't quite make me out. Why, I just hate to close an eyelid, when there's so much to take in. But I guess *she* goes off to sleep at about 11 o'clock every night, like she was at home in a London suburb."

Undoubtedly Margaret was right.

I am furious because Mrs. Pansy Baker has spoken in a faintly injured voice of the fact that we have had to share a bedroom. I have seen all along that this enforced intimacy is extraordinarily hard on me, but it hasn't really dawned on me yet that it's apparently extraordinarily hard on her as well. Now I perceive that it is, and am unjustly indignant.

As for the London suburb, it is all I can do not to invent and relate on the spot a legend about having recently bought Apsley House and gone to live in it.

I get out of the bus, and wonder what Margaret really meant, and try not to think that I now know.

MISS-BLAKE-AND-MISS-BOLTON

(1)

ON THE SHIP AT LONDON DOCKS,
where I first see them, Miss Blake and Miss Bolton
are talking about preventives against sea-sickness.
Miss Blake says, a little harshly:

"Well, Bolton, you know what you are. If necessary I shall force you to take a teaspoonful before
we're out of the river."

"Oh, I shall be all right. I think you ought to try
one of the cachets, honestly I do, because of that
head you had this morning."

"Oh, I shall be all right."

Their solicitude is entirely on behalf of one another. The manner of each is very curt and English.

They are seen off by two friends in nurses' uniform, who shake hands with them in a hearty mas-
culine kind of way and say: "Well, cheerioh" and:
"Give my love to Stalin"; and then walk away
down a long and rather dreary vista of dock which
is all composed of barrels and rusty iron rods and
piled-up wooden planks—bumping against one
another as they go.

And after all, nobody succumbs to sea-sickness. The sea is smooth all the way to Leningrad.

Miss Blake and Miss Bolton sit beside one another at meals, speaking very seldom. When they do utter, their remarks seem mysterious and disjointed.

"Did you write that postcard before we left the flat?"

"Yes, but I had to leave it for Miss M. to post."

"Oh, she'll be all right. She can do *that* sort of thing."

I hope to find out what are the sort of things that Miss M. can't do—but nothing more transpires.

Not till we have finished the *hors d'œuvres* (beetroot, tomatoes and sardines) and the fried fish, and are confronting the chops—rather pale and tough—do they speak again.

"What do you think of that book?"

"It's O.K. In a way."

"That's what I thought."

"Of course, I haven't finished it."

Miss Bolton accepts this in silence. She understands, better than I do, why Miss Blake hasn't finished the book, and whether she ever intends to finish it, and what she means when she says it's O.K. only in a way.

Once, Miss Blake speaks to me. I think she has only selected me, out of the eleven passengers on board, because I happen to be sitting exactly opposite to her in the dining-saloon.

"I see they've put little flags on the tables. I suppose we've got the Union Jack because we're English."

Shall I say: No, it must be mere coincidence? I don't.

"I should never have thought they'd do that," says Miss Blake.

Why would she never have thought so?

I should rather like to ask her, but Miss Bolton speaks — (their brief conversational impulses are always quite interdependent):

"They've got an American flag at the other end, where that American woman is sitting. And what's the blue-and-white one?"

Somebody thinks it's the Greek flag.

"But why? We're not any of us Greek. There's only that Armenian."

"Perhaps it was the nearest thing they could get."

[149]

On this profound thought, we sink into silence once more.

That is to say, the English sink into silence.

I can hear Mrs. Pansy Baker's Middle Western voice going gaily on and on at the other end of the table, disregarding the gloomy contradictions of the Canadian engineer, and I can hear the two Russian passengers talking both at once, quietly and without heat, about the poems of Pushkin. They have been talking about them since yesterday.

The ice-cream follows the cheese, and is very good and someone says that *all* the books are agreed about the excellence of Russian ice-cream. It will be the same everywhere we go, all over Russia.

"Blake," says Miss Bolton peremptorily at this, "whatever happens, I don't mean ever to buy mauve again. It fades."

"Even when there's no sun. So what it would do if there was," says Miss Blake—and there ends.

On the boat, there is nothing whatever to do. We stop once, at Holtenau, and a German girl gets off and is left standing rather forlornly on the dock in the middle of an enormous group of uniformed officials, having been given to understand that there is no train leaving until the following morning, that there is no accommodation available for the night, and that the station waiting-room is locked and cannot be unlocked.

We ask one another in tones of concern if she will be all right, and wave at her encouragingly, and then go on down the Kiel Canal and forget all about her.

Nor do I give her another thought until, weeks later, I meet Miss Blake and Miss Bolton at Kharkov after parting from them in Moscow, and quite suddenly, in a tram, Miss Bolton remarks:

"I wonder what happened to that German girl?"

And Miss Blake replies:

"I expect she was all right really."

(2)

Rather like a recurrent *motif* in a musical composition Miss Blake and Miss Bolton come and go throughout the phases of my Russian trip.

At Leningrad we are in separate hotels, but meet on the same excursions.

The same train takes us to Moscow but Miss Blake and Miss Bolton travel "soft" and I travel "hard." They come and visit me, very amiably, in the morning and enquire whether I "caught" anything in the night—as if I were a kind of nocturnal Isaak Walton.

They also ask rather wistfully about breakfast and I am in a position to confirm their worst suspicions. There is no official breakfast on the train at all.

When I asked the same question at the Leningrad Hotel the reply was that I should be able to have breakfast on arrival at Moscow.

"And what time *do* we arrive?"

"I cannot say."

"But *about* what time?"

"In the morning. It will not be so very late."

It may not seem very late, theoretically, to Intourist at Leningrad. To me, after waking for good at 6 o'clock, it seems very late long before nine—and Miss Blake and Miss Bolton assure me that they *know* we shan't reach Moscow before 10.28.

I have two apples in my bag, and I feel that I ought to offer to share them—and so I would if I wasn't certain that they'd accept. This first unhallowed thought gives place to something slightly less unworthy, and I think of Sir Philip Sydney,

[152]

and wonder how he could have done it, and feel that I've never really appreciated him before.

Suddenly a woman with a handkerchief over her head clatters down the corridor, carrying a huge kettle, and a basket full of glasses.

Tea.

We all three order tea enthusiastically, and I am sufficiently exhilarated to follow, though belatedly, the example of Sir Philip Sydney.

Miss Blake and Miss Bolton say No, no, to a share of the apples, but really mean Yes, yes, and presently we divide them—and very hard and sour they are.

"Do you remember Lyons?" says Miss Bolton significantly to Miss Blake.

"Yes. I do."

"We sometimes," Miss Bolton explains to me, "have a cup of tea at Lyons' Corner House."

I had guessed it.

"Hard"-class travelling has the merit of being less unnaturally stuffy than "soft" class where it is usually impossible to keep the window open because of the dust, and the door gives onto a corridor that is jammed with people, standing about or sitting on little seats that tip up against the wall.

In the "hard" class the wooden seats run the whole length of the coach, and above each one is another wooden plank, and above that another one again.

The Comrades, for the most part, have slept in their clothes, only removing their boots, Some of them have hired little pillows—which I know from experience to be as hard as bricks—and a cotton covering. Most of them use their luggage or their boots for pillows.

In the "soft" class, Miss Blake says, anybody leaving the carriage enquires politely if her neighbour intends to remain in it, so as to keep the luggage in view. Failing a neighbour, the door of the carriage should be shut and locked. In no circumstances, it seems, should luggage ever be left in a Russian train without a responsible eye on it.

"Who is looking after yours now?"

"We have two Russian women in with us. They *had* put two men, but we said they must change. So they did."

"But I think perhaps we ought to go and see about it, now," says Miss Bolton—skilfully bringing in her exit line, since, unless she does, there is

no particular reason why the conversation should
ever stop.

They leave me.

Miss Blake goes too.

They are evidently animated by one set of impulses only.

When we get to Moscow I lose them again. We
are drafted to separate hotels. Mrs. Pansy Baker
and I are at the same one, and the Canadian
engineer, and the Armenian who, after the first
two meals, disappears and is never seen again.

Perhaps he has been massacred?

Mrs. Pansy Baker and I each have a room to
ourselves this time and I perceive that in the
restaurant—which is a very large one, with a view
of the Kremlin—we are moved to select tables for
breakfast as far as possible from one another.

The Canadian engineer avoids us both.

I am, however, in the superior position of having
an English friend already in Moscow—or so I hope,
although a life-time seems to me to have elapsed
since he gave me, in London, a copy of his itinerary,
and assured me that he would reach Moscow from
the Crimea just before I reached it from Leningrad. He has even given me the name of his hotel.

I VISIT THE SOVIETS

It is as I go out into the streets of Moscow to find it, that I catch sight once more of Miss Blake and Miss Bolton striding, in the most purposeful way, just ahead of me.

They have begun sight-seeing already. How energetic they are! How earnest! One has a notebook and the other a camera.

A fragment of dialogue is wafted back to me just before they turn a corner.

"You ought to put the stalks in glycerine. I read it in the *Daily Sketch*."

"I think you're wrong, Blakie. It wasn't the *Daily Sketch*. It was the *Daily Mirror*. Because I remember, it was next to the picture of Useless Eustace."

"MOSCOU DÉVOILÉ"

(1)

TOURISTS, IN ALL THE INTOURIST hotels in all the principal towns of Soviet Russia, exchange the same fragments of conversation.

"Have you done Moscow yet?"

"No, I'm going there tomorrow night. I came in by Odessa. I've done Kharkov, and Rostov, and Kiev."

"Ah, then you're going out by sea from Leningrad. Unless you're flying from Moscow?"

"No, I shall be going by sea. Have you done Odessa and the South?"

"No, I've done the Caucasus. You should do the Caucasus. What is Odessa like?"

"Odessa is delightful. The hotel at Rostov was good, except for the cockroaches. The food was bad at Kharkov."

"Ah, there was a Frenchman here yesterday who'd just come from Kharkov, and *he* said the food wasn't good."

And at this gratifying coincidence everybody looks pleased.

I VISIT THE SOVIETS

Sometimes it is a little like the survivors of a shipwreck meeting on a fragment of desert island.

"Are you still all right for soap?"

"Yes, I shall just last out till Kiev. What about you?"

"Oh, I'm all right. I brought a great deal. But my ink is pretty low."

"There's an American lady who can let you have ink. She gave me some in Leningrad and she's coming on here. She had safety-pins too."

"How marvellous! Perhaps she'd like some soda mints or aspirins. I have heaps of those."

"I dare say. Or Keatings. Or perhaps you could lend her a book."

People part at Moscow and meet again, sometimes most unwillingly, at Yalta. They ask one another how they have been getting on, and if they met the French astronomer, and the English journalist, and the noisy young Finns with the portable gramophone. Those who met at Leningrad, and were in the same train coming from Moscow, and parted gracefully at Tiflis only to be once more confronted with one another at Gorki, are bound by some unwritten law to sit at the same table for meals. I often wonder whether they really like to

[158]

do this, or if they just feel obliged to do it, for old sake's sake. But this is in my early days. Later on, I fall under the same spell, and the question is answered.

In Moscow, I meet Peter—but not as one meets stray French astronomers and English journalists and gramophone-playing Finns. It is a meeting that was arranged—incredibly, as it now seems— in Bloomsbury, some four months ago. I have had the name of his hotel, and the dates when he expects to be there, in my diary ever since I left England.

His dates have been altered—so have mine—all knowledge of him is denied at the Metropole Hotel, where he ought to be and Intourist tells me: (1) that there are no letters for me and no messages, (2) that if there were I couldn't have them because it is a Day of Rest.

It is anything but a Day of Rest for me, whatever it may be for Moscow.

I have travelled all night, and walked about looking for Peter half the day, and I have not yet got used to having my luncheon between 3 and 5 o'clock in the afternoon, and the hotel to which I have been sent is on one side of the Red Square—

which no trams traverse—and everything else in Moscow is on the other side.

All the same, the Red Square is very beautiful, and they are quite right to allow no trams there. In the evening I walk across it once more, and admire the huge walls and towers of the Kremlin, and the long row of fir-trees against the grey stone, and the pure, beautiful lines of the Lenin Mausoleum, perfectly placed before the great fort, and the strange, Byzantine domes and whorls and minarets of the ancient Basil Cathedral.

Sentinels with fixed bayonets guard the Mausoleum, and there are long, long queues of people—they must number hundreds—waiting to pass inside. From the top of the Kremlin flutters the Red Flag, and from somewhere beneath it a light strikes upward, so that the brave scarlet colour shows as plainly against the clear evening sky as it did in the morning sunlight.

One walks across the Red Square more safely than anywhere else in Moscow. Not as regards one's feminine virtue—*that*, I think, would be safe anywhere in Russia, were I a quarter of my present age and as alluring as Venus—but simply as regards life and limb.

I VISIT THE SOVIETS

Everywhere else, the traffic is shattering, and the Comrades, running for their lives in every direction—as well they may—are a menace. So are the trams, which bucket along on uneven rails and draw up with a slow jerk which gives a misleading impression altogether. One feels that here are deliberate, rather uncertain trams, that may very likely require a good strong push from somebody before starting at all.

And on the contrary, hardly have they stopped and hardly have hundreds of Comrades fought their way out of them, than a bell clangs and they start off again, leaving hundreds more biting and kicking and pushing their way inside, hanging on the step and very often being violently shoved off it again.

The tram question—one of the less picturesque and endearing characteristics of the new régime—is complicated in Moscow by the reconstructions that are going on everywhere. Whole streets are lying more or less inside-out, caverns yawn in the middle of roads, scaffolding suddenly blocks up pavements, and irrelevant-seeming pyramids of earth and loose stones and rubble rise up in quite unexpected places.

The trams do their gallant best, and often remind me of the story of Jules Verne in which the driver of a passenger train negotiated a precipice by going full-steam ahead and causing the train to jump the chasm. The trams, too, do something like that, but even so, they have to make colossal *détours*, and every few days their route is, without any warning, altered because the old route has become impassable.

In Leningrad there were hardly any cars. In Moscow there are a great many, and they all go hell-for-leather, and make a point of only sounding their horns at the very last minute when the lives of the walking Comrades positively hang by a thread.

In Moscow, as in Leningrad, people throng the streets. They keep on walking; they are like Felix the Cat. The Intourist guides, as usual, point out how purposeful they all are, how they walk with an object. One guide, more honest or less well-trained than the others, tells me that the housing shortage is very acute, and so perhaps it is more agreeable to spend one's free time in the street rather than in the home. A kind of Scylla or Charybdis.

I VISIT THE SOVIETS

These grim impressions dawn upon me little by little as I cross the Red Square, for perhaps the fourth time in twenty-four hours, to make another assault on the Metropole and Peter.

To my own unbounded astonishment, I am successful. There *is* a note from Peter. It has, I have no doubt, been there all along. It says that he is at the National Hotel. Have I got to cross the Red Square all over again? It is very beautiful, but I don't seem to care about crossing it again just yet.

I haven't got to. The National Hotel is only a few hundred yards from the Metropole.

If Peter and I were in London, I should not run, like an excited hare, up four flights of stairs to his bedroom. Old friends as we are, I shouldn't scream aloud with joy at the sight of him, nor he at the sight of me. In Moscow, however, we do all these things. We behave, in a word, almost like two foreigners.

And we talk and we talk and we talk.

Our impressions of Soviet Russia, most fortunately, coincide.

We have had identical experiences with fleas, guides, indiscreet indulgence in Russian bread, and the non-arrival of letters from home.

I VISIT THE SOVIETS

We offer one another soap, biscuits, Bromo and soda-mints. It is almost like two Eastern potentates exchanging gifts, especially when Peter generously says that I shall have his clothes-brush when he leaves—I forgot to pack mine—and I, in return, gracefully offer to wash his pocket-handkerchiefs when I do my own. And I stay and have supper with him—at about 11 P.M.—and at 1 o'clock in the morning cross the Red Square once more. This time I time myself, and find that it takes me, from door to door, a quarter of an hour.

It takes me a quarter of an hour, at home, to walk to the village post office, which is said to be a mile from the house.

At this rate, I shall be covering quite a number of miles every day in Moscow.

My bedroom window overlooks the river. I am pleased about it, until I notice that a particularly zealous form of reconstruction is taking place on the bank, and that Comrades in vast numbers are operating a huge drill. They are a night-shift, and a kind of *mieux de la mort* overtakes them at 2 in the morning, when they evolve a special series of noises, indicative of terrific energy. Then it all dies away, and the next shift doesn't begin till 7 o'clock.

I VISIT THE SOVIETS

(2)

Peter is under the auspices of an organization which takes an interest in literary tourists and the Organization is very kind to him, and gives him theatre tickets, and special facilities, and a guide all to himself. These benefits he shares with me.

I am secretly terrified of the guide, who is youngish, and very tough, and has a swivel eye. She has lived in the United States, and says that she once hiked from Denver, Colorado, to California. It can't have been half as exhausting as hiking from one end of Moscow to the other, which is our daily achievement.

We visit museums, and picture galleries, and crèches, and factories, and schools and clinics. We see, at a rough estimate, a hundred thousand busts of Lenin and ninety thousand pictures of Stalin.

The guide has a curious habit of walking us briskly along over the cobbles, round such bits of reconstruction as lie in our way, for some time, and then abruptly stopping while she asks a passer-by the way to wherever she is taking us. This always turns out to be in some quite opposite direction to the one in which we are going. All is à refaire, and we turn round and begin all over again.

The result, not unnaturally, is that we always arrive late for our appointments.

"The Little Monster has no sense of time," says Peter—this being the endearing *sobriquet* by which he refers to the guide.

"None at all. She arrived three-quarters of an hour late to fetch us from the hotel."

"And then she took us the wrong way."

"She evidently hasn't any bump of locality at all. Some people haven't," I say—having the best of reasons for knowing what I am talking about.

Peter only replies, not unjustifiably, that to have no sense of time and no sense of direction seems to him a poor equipment with which to set up as a guide.

Sometimes we board a tram together. It is invariably bunged to the roof with pale, grimy, heavily-built Comrades, too tightly jammed together for strap-hanging to be necessary, or even possible. No one ever sits down. There are people sitting, when one gets in, but I think it is because they have got wedged there and can't move.

On one occasion the Little Monster, startlingly and suddenly, says in my ear:

The tram is invariably bunged to the roof with pale, grimy, heavily built Comrades. I often think of the Black Hole of Calcutta.

I VISIT THE SOVIETS

"A pregnant woman may go in the front part of the tram, where there is more room. It is a law."

I wonder whether she thinks I am going to make a fraudulent attempt to take advantage of this concession. But I don't. I remain where I am, leaning heavily on the shoulder of a man in a blouse, with somebody's portfolio digging into the small of my back, and an enormous female Comrade grasping my elbow with one hand and wiping the sweat off her face with the other.

I often think of the Black Hole of Calcutta.

The tram jerks, and jolts, and stops, and more people get in, and the Little Monster—who isn't more than five feet high—disappears from view altogether. This time I think of the House of Stone in *The Four Feathers* and how those who fell down there never got up again. A mind well stored with literary references is said to be a great comfort to the possessor. I think my references must be of the wrong kind.

Peter, who is a large young man and stands like the Rock of Gibraltar in the tram, is much more of a comfort to me than any number of literary references. He always knows when to get out, which I never do, and the guide seldom.

Getting out of the tram is a very tense and difficult business. Every inch of the way has to be fought for, and there is always a sporting chance that the tram will start again before the people in front of one will let one go through, or the people behind one have ceased to try and push past. I carry a bruise on one ankle for days, where one of the more impetuous Comrades has given me a vigorous kick, in order that I should get out of his way.

I ask Peter if he knew about the pregnant women going in the front of the train, and he says Yes, but he doesn't see how they're to get there. Neither do I, unless they confide their pretty secret to the conductor and he or she passes it on to all the Comrades in the tram and a way is cleared. (Like Charlotte Brontë when she went to a party, and everybody stood up and made way for her.)

"We might ask the Little Monster," Peter suggests. Any delicacy which either of us has ever possessed at home, has long since left us. There are no inhibitions in Russia.

It is in a spirit of simple *camaraderie* that he and

I VISIT THE SOVIETS

I and the Little Monster go together to a clinic for the welfare of mothers and babies—actually a most excellent institution, admirably organized —and are given much full and intelligent physiological information, with Lenin—aged three— looking benevolently down on us from the wall.

As there is practically no wall in Moscow from which I have *not* seen Lenin looking down— either as an infant or as an elderly man exhorting the workers—there is no intervening stage—I have ceased to notice him consciously, but on this occasion I prefer him to the other pictures with which the walls are covered.

I prefer him to the unwholesome-looking red and blue maps of the human organism.

I prefer him to the things in bottles on a shelf.

I prefer him, a thousand times, to the master-piece which the woman doctor who is showing us round has kept to the last.

"This tumour is one of the largest we have ever . . ."

I say it is interesting—which I suppose it is, if I could bring myself to look at it, which I can't—and Peter says nothing. I think he is stunned. He is looking with a fixed, unnatural

[169]

intensity at an artificial tomato, carrot, apple and beetroot in a little case. Necessary items in the diet of infants, says the notice.

I think, perhaps, if one had seen all this—not the tumour, which *can't* be essential to anybody's education except a medical student's—but all the maps, and the photographs, and the measurements and the instructions—at a very much earlier age, before one had grown squeamish and when one's curiosity was young and strong, it might have been a very good thing.

It *does* give vital information, and it does give it in a scientific impersonal way, and it does stress the importance of bodily hygiene.

"Are school children ever brought here, to be taught physiological and biological facts?"

"Yes, often. They come in groups."

The last piece of information is superfluous. The Comrades, especially the school children, go everywhere in gorups. They are taught from the very beginning to lead the collective life.

Peter and I agree that the mother-and-babies Welfare Clinic is one of the best things we have seen in the Soviet Union, and that we approve of the visits there of the school children—with a mental reservation excluding the tumour.

From the Clinic the Little Monster takes us—going first in the wrong direction but afterwards recovering herself—to the Court of Marriages and Divorces. It consists of a bureau in a little room, with a middle-aged woman in charge, and two plants that look like indiarubber plants in pots in the doorway, each tied up with a pale, frail bow of papery white ribbon—like the ghosts of dead bridal decorations.

There are, as usual, Comrades sitting about and waiting and the guide says that they have either come to register their marriage or to get a divorce. They all look to me equally unexhilarated, and nearly all of them are holding small children.

A young Russian is at the bureau, and has said something, and it has been written down in a ledger, and he has, in his Russian way, settled down onto a hard-looking stool as if for life.

"He has just got a divorce," says the guide, and she asks him a great many questions about his private affairs, and translates his answers. (I am, and always have been, thoroughly aghast at the way in which private individuals are turned inside-out for the benefit of tourists—but I am bound to say that they never seem to raise any objection.)

It seems that the young Russian is not pleased with his wife. She reproaches him, rather strangely, with spending his money on amusements and on presents for her. It makes her, she complains, into a slave. They quarrel. He has, without telling her anything about it, got a divorce. When she reproaches him this evening, because he wishes to take her out to a cinema or a café, he will simply confront her with the *fait accompli*.

"It is very simple," says the Little Monster, looking unspeakably superior. She knows that in Capitalist countries nothing, least of all divorce, is as simple as that.

"Are marriages equally simple?"

"Yes, they are. This couple, with the two children, have come to register their marriage."

The husband with the divorce smiles at us very amiably and makes way for the couple with the two children. Some people might think that it is a little late in the day for them to come and register their marriage. But the guide, after the usual spate of questions and answers, is able to explain it all.

They have been eight years together. If they should get tired of one another, and decide to separate, it will be very much simpler to make arrangements for the welfare of the children if the marriage has been registered.

So here they are.

The whole thing—barring the questions of the guide and her translations of the replies to us— takes about five minutes.

We have witnessed a wedding in Moscow.

I wonder, sentimentally, whether the woman— who is sufficiently middle-aged to remember the old days—gives a thought to a new dress, and music, and flowers and a wedding-party.

I don't suppose she does. I see her grasp one child by the hand, and the husband takes the other, and they depart, without so much as a vestige of Mendelssohn's Wedding March to encourage them.

Peter—who collects information much more assiduously than I do—asks intelligent questions, and enters the answers in a little book, and the woman at the bureau—I suppose she is the Registrar?—is very obliging and only breaks off once or twice to divorce or marry a few people who drift in and out.

It is 1 o'clock.

[173]

I VISIT THE SOVIETS

We can go to the Organization that supplied us with the Little Monster, where Peter wants to ask about theatre tickets. It is all on the way to his hotel.

It isn't on the way to my hotel, but then nothing is—except the Red Square. How well I shall know it all before I leave Moscow—the Kremlin, the fir-trees, the Mausoleum, the Basil Cathedral. . . . How well I seem to know it all already, for that matter. I go past them in the morning, on my way sight-seeing, and I go past them after 3 or 4 or 5 o'clock luncheon with Peter, and I very often go past them, once each way, before and after the theatre, or the cinema, or just supper. My final view of them is usually at 2 o'clock in the morning.

Well, they are very beautiful.

Still, I do sometimes wonder if there will ever be any taxis in Moscow.

Peter and I sit at a table in the National Hotel. (His.) He has surplus meal-tickets, and lets me take advantage of them handsomely, so that I get second-class meals instead of the third-class ones to which alone I am really entitled.

I VISIT THE SOVIETS

We have ordered our food and settled down for the forty minutes' wait that will precede its arrival. We have told one another what we think of the picture-gallery, the tomb of Lenin, the Workers' Club, and the offices of *Pravda*—all visited today —and we have angrily wondered why we are never sent to the theatre, not even to see *Romeo and Juliet*, without a guide to make sure we understand what it's all about.

On a less cultural level, I have told Peter about the unknown lady whom I met downstairs in the lavatories, and who looked at me so sadly and said, without preliminary, "Dieu! ça sent mauvais ici!" and walked away sighing. He has told me about his difficulties in connection with getting his boots cleaned. We have discussed, by no means for the first time, the dinner that we propose to have together at the Berkeley when—sometimes I feel it ought to be *if*—we get back to London again.

After the *bortsch* has come, and restored us, we are able to rise to a higher plane, and become literary.

"What will your book about Russia be called, Peter?"

"I haven't yet decided. What will yours?"

[175]

"I don't know. I've thought of several names. I may just call it 'Harpers' Surprise.' "

"?"

"Harpers are my American publishers, and it was they who sent me here, to write a book about Russia. I think they'll be so surprised, when they see that I haven't really got any facts or figures in it at all."

Peter assures me that several other people have written books about Russia, filled with facts and figures, and tells me to look at the Webbs. I had much better not try to emulate the Webbs.

I agree.

"Sometimes I think I might just call the book 'Me and the Soviet'—or 'The Comrades and I.' Of course, in the old days, books about Russia had fine romantic names."

"*A Life for the Tsar,*" says Peter.

"*The Exiles of Siberia.*"

"*Nuits de Moscou,*" or was that the name of a waltz?

I am not sure.

But I think that I shall combine romance and realism and perhaps call my book about Russia "*Moscou dévoile.*" That will be faintly reminiscent of the *Contes d'Hoffmann*, and yet give me plenty of scope for saying what I think about Moscow.

For there is no doubt that Moscow, whether through its fault or my own, has a most depressing effect on me. I think it's partly the number of comrades who walk the streets and throng the trams and stand in queues outside the shops and the cinemas, all looking rather drab and unwashed and solemn. And one has caught such depressing glimpses, through unshaded windows, of dormitories with beds packed like sardines. Besides, it is never exhilarating to see such quantities of wholesale destruction going on as is necessitated by the Soviet determination to make a completely new city of Moscow.

I quite see that wonders have been achieved in a very short time. I haven't any doubt that the condition of the workers, before the Revolution, was abominable beyond description. I haven't really any serious doubts that they are working towards a better state of things than they have ever known.

But I have a *bourgeois* longing to see gaily dressed shop windows—and perhaps gaily-dressed people in the streets as well — and to see more

[177]

individualism and less collectivism — and, in a word, there seems to me to be a total absence of *fun*, in Moscow.

Beauty, there is. In some of the buildings that have survived, in the Ballet, in the Gallery of Western Art, in many of the theatre productions. *Romeo and Juliet* was a beautiful production. So was *Eugene Onegin* at the Opera.

Probably I have come to Moscow in quite the wrong spirit. I am making the mistake of comparing its newly-begun institutions — of which, God wot, I have seen plenty of examples — with similar institutions in England and in America. Absurd and unreasonable.

The Soviet institutions—clinics, welfare centres, schools, crèches, hospitals — are all working under difficulties, and are all hampered by lack of experience and lack of appliances. (They handicap themselves still further by a cast-iron determination to accept no outside criticism whatever and by assuming that perfection has already been achieved, which is far from being the case.)

A recollection—inaccurate, as usual—comes to my mind of some uncivil aphorism of Dr. Johnson's about women writing books, or pursuing any

[178]

other intellectual avocation.

"It is like a dog that walks upon its hind legs, Sir. We do not ask whether the thing be well or ill done. The wonder is that it should be done at all." I am sure that I had better remember about Dr. Johnson and the dog, when I try to collect my impressions of Soviet Russia.

At 11 o'clock at night an American acquaintance of Peter's appears and suggests taking us to pay a call on a man who writes books—a Swede. He has said that he will be at home between 12 and 1 A.M.

He isn't, and we all settle down in his kitchen—situated on the staircase, and which he shares with five other families in the same building—and wait for his arrival.

At a quarter to 1 he comes, bringing three friends—a woman and two men.

We all sit in the bed-sitting room and talk. There ought to be a *samovar*, but there isn't. Only a wireless. I think my ideas are out of date.

The conversation is about the law concerning Abortion — (naturally) — the new Metro, a poet who has annoyed the Government by one of his poems and has been sent as a punishment to work at the construction of a new bridge across the Neva—where he will surely be of no use whatever —and the state of literature in England.

I do not join in this intelligently. For one thing I am getting sleepy, and for another, nobody has ever heard of me as a writer in Russia — and wouldn't be interested if they had—as none of my works is political or sociological—so nobody refers to me. Just as I am thinking that with any luck nobody will notice it if I do go to sleep, my host abruptly enquires of me which writer of fiction is leading the younger school in England now? Which indeed?

I must think of a name, and I must try and think of one that will convey something to my hearers into the bargain.

I hope to combine a modicum of truth with a certain amount of diplomacy by saying, "Dreiser."

"Theodore Dreiser?"

"Theodore Dreiser," I repeat firmly, and I really think I have displayed great presence of mind, considering that I am more than half asleep.

"I meant," says my host, "which of the moderns. Theodore Dreiser is the literature of the grandmothers, yes?"

Not of any of the grandmothers *I* know, he isn't. But I don't say so. Theodore Dreiser and I retire, together, into the ranks of the grandmothers and are disinterred no more.

Only just before we go away, at three o'clock, the only other woman present asks me rather sharply if I have any silk stockings, aspirins, lipsticks, cotton frocks or nail-scissors to sell.

I suppose she thinks it's all I'm fit for—and I am disposed to agree with her, and make a rendezvous for next day, for her to come to my hotel and inspect my belongings.

Shortly afterwards, I say good-night to Peter at his door and continue on my way—Red Square, Kremlin, Mausoleum, fir-trees, Basil Cathedral, Old Uncle Tom Cobley and all, Old Uncle Tom Cobley and all.

(3)

The Russian lady keeps her word. She much more than keeps it. She not only comes and buys everything that I want to sell, but swoops down on a large number of things that I *don't* want to sell, and says she'll take them, as well. She opens my wardrobe and takes down my frocks, she lifts up the pillow on my bed by a sort of unerring instinct —like a water-diviner—and discloses my pyjamas, and she looks inside my sponge-bag. (What can she possibly suppose that I am hiding inside my sponge-bag?)

"Look, I take this ink-bottle off of you, as well, and if you have a fountain-pen I take that, and I take for my husband the blue frame—(he will not want the photograph, besides it is your children, you will like to keep it)—and for myself I take those things what I have already bought, and the red jumper, the pyjamas, the two frocks. Have you any boiled sweets?"

No, I haven't any boiled sweets. And nothing will induce me to part with the safety ink-bottle, or the blue frame, or my only two frocks.

It takes a long while to convince the Russian lady that I really mean this, and I have eventually to concede the red jumper and the pyjamas. She still looks so fixedly at the ink-bottle that I become unnerved, and distract her by an offer of meat-juice tablets—for her husband—and handker-chiefs and safety-pins for herself.

She buys them all, and pays me in roubles on

the spot. When I put the money away in my bag she says she will buy the bag, and when I hastily thrust the bag into my suitcase she says she will buy the suitcase.

I get her out of the room at last by giving her a lip-stick as a sort of bonus, like a pound of tea for a cash sale.

When, in the passage outside, I refer to our morning's work she says Hush! Not so loud—and I realize that the whole transaction has been an illicit one, and that Comrade Stalin would disapprove. We might perhaps even find ourselves, like the ill-conducted poet, constructing a new bridge across the Neva.

All the same, if I'd known what a shortage there is of pretty, brightly-coloured odds and ends in the Soviet Republic, I think I should have brought a great many more of them with me—and not only for the sake of turning a doubtfully honest rouble out of them, either.

One morning Peter and I go to Kolominsky escorted by the Little Monster. She says it is an ancient monastery, and when we get there it *looks* like an ancient monastery, but she recants, and says it was a Palace of Ivan the Terrible. I don't know

[183]

which she means but prefer to think of it as a monastery.

Much the most peaceful spot I have seen in Russia—no Comrades, no reconstruction, not even a picture of Lenin with outstretched arm and clenched fist.

Just as I am sitting on a stone wall under the lime-trees and looking down at the fields and the river, the guide tells me that on this exact spot Ivan the Terrible used to watch the peasants being flogged.

It is a great pity she cannot let well alone.

However, it is today that we hear her, for the first and last time, make a joke. On the way back to the tram, passing through a tiny village, we see a little calf lying on the roadside, with a small pig nuzzling affectionately against it, both of them fast asleep in the sunshine.

Even the swivel eye of the Little Monster softens as she gazes down at them, and she says:

"Look! In a Socialist state—no prejudice!"

For the moment, as we all three laugh, she seems quite human.

It doesn't last.

She becomes as hortatory and tiresome as ever

long before the tram has lurched back into Moscow with us, and makes us get off at the wrong stop so that we have to walk several additional miles to Peter's hotel.

"It still seems odd to be lunching at 4 o'clock."

"Yes, doesn't it? Shall you have *bortsch* again today?"

"Yes, I like it."

"How fortunate you are. But their fish is better than their meat, and the ice-cream is good."

"Excellent. Much, much better than the *compote*."

"Oh, the *compote*——!"

We do not describe the *compote* to one another. It is not necessary, as we have met it, both here and in Leningrad, at every meal. We know all about the rather tough acid little fruits in the top of the glass dish, and the sliced apple below, and the two rather consoling little bits of tinned apricot at the very bottom. Curious how very much one seems to think and talk about one's food in Moscow.

Also one's drink.

The mineral water is good, but expensive. The ordinary, plain water—what, in any other country, would be the drinking-water—arrives on the table boiled. And very well-advised, too. But either the boiling, or its own natural properties, have turned it pale yellow, and given it a strange smell, and a very peculiar taste. The remaining alternative, since neither of us drinks wine, and the beer — which is excellent—is a ruinous price and we can't often run to it—is tea in a glass.

Everybody in England said to me before I came away:

"Oh, you'll get used to tea with lemon. You'll end by loving it."

I don't love it yet—but perhaps I haven't been trying long enough. I come nearer to loving it—not very near, but still, nearer—when it is quite plain, without sugar or lemon or anything.

Meals, it is scarcely necessary to say, take a very long time in Russia. Hours elapse between the moment of sitting down, and detaching from its book the coupon that represents food, and the moment when the waiter comes to take one's order. Hours more between each course. (The coupon entitles one to three courses. I have never tried asking for a second helping, but I don't think the coupon would run to it.)

I VISIT THE SOVIETS

The tea comes at the very end, and is always much too hot to drink, and so necessitates another long wait.

Sometimes Peter and I talk like the thoughtful and intelligent people we really are, and discuss Socialism, and Communism, and tell each other that we *really* ought to have seen Russia *before* the Revolution, in order to judge of the vast improvement effected. (When Peter says this to me, it is very reasonable. When I say it to him, it is simply idiotic, as before the Revolution he was an infant in the nursery.)

Sometimes we discuss our neighbours.

"I saw that man over there when I was in Batum. He speaks Dutch."

"Does he? Yes, he looks as though he might. There are some Germans at my hotel. They've made friends with Mrs. Pansy Baker and she went with them to see an abortion clinic and a boot factory."

"What fun. There's Capablanca. He's playing in the chess tournament."

"I hope he'll win, I like his head. Have you seen a single pretty woman yet, in Russia?"

"No. Have you?"

[187]

"No."

Once, when a blonde with black eyelashes and a tightly-fitting white frock comes in and sits down all by herself at the table next to ours, Peter hisses at me through his teeth:

"If ever there was one, I'll take my oath that's one of what we know there aren't any of in Russia!"

I understand him perfectly.

In Russia, now, we have repeatedly been told, there are no prostitutes.

They have all been collected, and placed in a sort of Home of Rest, like aged horses in England.

It is, I believe, possible to go and visit them. I suppose, if we ever do, they will be expected to answer any indiscreet question that any of us may, through the guide, elect to ask them.

I think, on the whole, I won't visit the prostitutes.

Sometimes Peter and I just talk about England, and Hartland Quay, and the Fourth of June at Eton, and people we both know in London or Devonshire. It feels like looking back into another life, and on those occasions—which are generally in the small hours of the morning after a gruelling day of trams, Comrades, museums, clinics and factories—I go past the Kremlin, the fir-trees and the Mausoleum without so much as noticing them. And that, as a matter of fact, nearly brings my whole career to an end, because I also omit to notice the blue light that suddenly flashes out above the entrance to the Kremlin, and is meant as a warning to the Red Square in general that a car, containing a member of the Government, is about to emerge. And so, to the dramatic clanging of a bell, it does—shooting out with inconceivable rapidity between the sentries, and swerving madly away into the distance.

The Government is afraid, someone tells me, that without these precautions some of its members may be assassinated.

It is not afraid, evidently, of itself assassinating any of the pedestrians who may be unable to get out of the way of the car quickly enough.

More than once, I am nearly assassinated myself. However, I escape and go on down the hill, and past the reconstruction on the river-bank, where the drill is hard at it, and into the hotel.

The dining-room is brightly lit, and full of people, and a little orchestra is playing "Sous les Toits de Paris"—as it does nightly.

[189]

I look in as I go by.

Mrs. Pansy Baker is at a table with her Germans, talking to them very earnestly. She is saying: "I have had a sad life."

I think this must be the beginning of a reference to Mr. Baker.

Very likely he, too, has had a sad life.

Quite a lot of new people have come, and the Swedish pedagogue has disappeared. Perhaps, however, he is only out to dinner.

In my bedroom is one cockroach. I don't like it at all. But it is headed towards the door, which I civilly hold open for it, and out it goes. A lull in the reconstruction work has set in, and I think what a good moment this will be in which to go to sleep.

The orchestra, now playing something very odd that I keep on thinking I know but can't identify, is nothing.

Sometimes I win this nightly race with the reconstruction, sometimes I don't.

Tonight it has only *reculé pour mieux sauter*. And they have got quite a new tool to work with— something like a hammer, dropping slowly down a flight of steps, over and over again, one step at a time. At last it drops once too often, and they don't pick it up again.

We are back once more at "*Sous les Toits de Paris.*"

Sur les lits de Moscou . . .

(4)

It is a black day for me when Peter leaves Moscow, in order to achieve first Leningrad and then England. I know that I am going to miss him dreadfully, and that I wish I was going home myself, and that instead I've got to stay on in Russia for an incredible number of weeks, doing things I don't want to do.

I think of Mark Tapley in the swamps at Eden, with fever and rattlesnakes, and of Mrs. Trollope, also in America, trying to force fancy pin-cushions on unwilling buyers. At least I haven't got to do that—and if I had, it would be much easier for me than for Mrs. Trollope, because the Russians—unlike the Americans—would certainly buy them.

We go up and say goodbye to the literary Organization, and thank them for all their kindness, including the services of the guide, and we ask for the guide, in order to say goodbye to her too, but she is coy and remains invisible. I don't think she really liked us much. It seems natural to me that *we* didn't like *her*, but extraordinary to a degree that *she* shouldn't have liked *us*.

A book is produced, and we are invited to sign our distinguished names in it, beneath our impressions of Soviet Russia.

I don't think that complete sincerity is the hallmark of either of our efforts. Neither is the ready zeal with which we take down the full address of the Organization, and undertake to write, and send copies of our books when written.

There is a final expedition to collect the films that Peter has had to have developed in Moscow before he can take them out of the country, and for which he has to pay colossal sums. On the way, we try—as often before—to enter a neglected-looking church, but the doors, as always, are padlocked, and when I look through the keyhole— as I always do on principle—everything inside is falling to pieces.

I don't think the Russians are telling the truth, when they say that some churches are still kept open as churches, and that the people can go to them if they want to. If so, they must be in remarkably inaccessible parts of Moscow.

"Look!" says Peter.

Over one door, in a very shabby street where all the paint is peeling off all the houses and huge holes gape between all the cobble-stones, is a doorway with stone bas-reliefs above it of the English Lion and the Unicorn.

There is something odd about them. . . .

I see what it is.

The crown has been conscientiously chipped away, and the Lion and the Unicorn are pawing forlornly at nothing.

Peter and I agree, rather solemnly, that the Soviet is certainly very *thorough*.

In the evening, in the deepest dejection, I go and see him off at the station.

In another two days I shall be going away myself, to Rostov. I am glad of it. I remind myself irresistibly, just now, of the title of a French book I used to be made to read aloud at school: *L'Orpheline de Moscou*. I am not an *orpheline*—and if I were, should be no more pitiable than the Major-General of the *Pirates of Penzance* in the same predicament—but that is how I feel.

[193]

I VISIT THE SOVIETS

"Goodbye, Peter. Don't forget to post all my letters and ring up my family."

"I won't forget. Goodbye, Elizabeth."

Nothing remains for me but the Red Square, the Kremlin, Mausoleum, fir-trees, Basil Cathedral—and the drill on the river-bank at the end of it all.

MR. FAIRCHILD IN MOSCOW

WHATEVER I MAY HAVE EXPECTED TO find in Russia, I never expected the Fairchild Family. It gives me a kind of shock, of mingled astonishment, home-sickness, pleasure and amusement, when I see the familiar purple-grey binding of an edition which is so absurdly well known to me that I have no need at all to look for the title in gilt letters on the backs of the twin volumes. (Only there ought to be three.)

It is the Fairchild family.

Papa, Mamma, Lucy, Emily and Henry and the faithful John, and equally faithful (but hasty-tempered) Betty.

It is an early edition—a third. Not, unfortunately, the first, in which is enshrined the curious incident of Mr. Fairchild taking his young family to see a corpse in a neighbouring cottage, where "the stink was extremely powerful even before they reached the door"—an incident which never, I think, went beyond the first edition.

But it is a very nice edition, and in perfect condition, steel engravings and all.

Inside each cover is a book-plate, a crest and

motto beneath a crown, and "Graf Lamsdorf" in Russian lettering.

On the opposite page is written in copperplate, with pale violet ink: Mary. And the writing tells me that it was inscribed many, many years ago—I think long before I was born.

Was the Graf a nobleman of the old régime, and had he a daughter called Mary to whom her English governess gave the Fairchild family as a reward for diligence—or perhaps as a present at Christmas? Or did the governess—the Miss—bring one or two treasured volumes of her own childhood out to Russia with her, and read them aloud to the children when they had been good at their English lessons? If so, it was she who was "Mary."

What happened to the first volume?

How did volumes two and three come into the shelf of Russian text-books where I find them, in a book-shop in Moscow? They've been there a long while, judging from the dust on them.

Perhaps the Graf and his family escaped during the Revolution, and had to leave everything behind them, but found that in some odd way a book or two had survived, and that volume one of the Fairchild family was amongst them.

[196]

Perhaps the Miss was sent home, to the English rectory in Somersetshire, for a holiday, and the first volume found its way into her luggage and she thought, of course, she was going back to her Russian pupils, and the sleigh-rides, and the skating, and the odd, late hours—and she must remember to look for volumes two and three and send them back to her own little nieces, who were getting old enough to enjoy story-books.

And then she never did go back.

The book opens, all of itself, in my hands.

"O dear, dear mamma, this is like old days again! If papa only were here, I could almost fancy that time was gone back, and that we were setting off to our dear hut in the wood."

How well I remember that speech of poor dear Lucy's, made shortly after the whole of the family had been translated from a small (but Christian) home to "a fine property and large house near Reading" with a hatchment, or escutcheon for the dead, above its pillared portico, to welcome them on arrival.

Yes, they are all at the Grove now, and a few pages further back Henry is taking his celebrated plunge into the pigs'-wash, and being upheld by his "stout nankeen frock" and the exertions of Mrs. Tilney, the lady's-maid.

A good deal further on, Miss Bessy Goodriche, the giddy, will scatter over the pages her favourite ejaculation—La!—and the intolerable Louisa will have introduced Emily to the pomps and vanities of Lady Catherine Tollemache's archery meeting.

Yes, here she is—just as I thought, poor Emily.

"The white frock the child wore was a mass of frills, diminishing gradually in size to her waist: her petticoats were short, fully displaying her ankles. The velvet spencer, from its length of waist, absolutely divided her little figure in two: her black sash was tied in front instead of behind, and her bonnet was profusely trimmed within as well as without. A delicate pair of lavender gloves, sewed with black, completed her costume, save that, in her little way, she was as much starched and bustled out as Louisa."

O Emily, Emily! How very fortunate for you it is that your excellent papa is still away from home. What would he not have to say about the natural proneness of the human heart to wickedness and vanity!

Except from Emily's point of view, there isn't

enough of Mr. Fairchild, in volume three. I've always thought there wasn't enough of him in volume three. He doesn't punish any of the children, he hardly ever rebukes them, he has nothing to say about the besetting sins of his neighbours, he spends most of his time away from home, advising old Mrs. Goodriche about the mending of her chimney-stack.

And now Mr. Fairchild and I meet in Moscow.

Even St. Petersburg, in the old pre-Revolution days, would have been the wrong setting for Mr. Fairchild. He would have been obstinately determined, I think, to instruct and enlighten the ignorant *moujiks*, and he would have deplored their inability to understand him when he spoke to them in English. (We know that Mr. Fairchild was at home with Latin and Greek, because he began to impart the rudiments of these languages to Henry when Henry was four. I think he probably knew a little French also—but certainly no Russian.) In the company of the nobility, he would have fared a little better—but not much. He would have thought them worldly and godless—and to think, with Mr. Fairchild, was to rebuke. The Russian nobility, unlike the *moujiks*, would have

[199]

understood his English only too well, and might have resented it.

Mr. Fairchild might well have ended by finding himself in the dungeons of the Kremlin.

As for Mr. Fairchild in present-day Moscow, I refuse to think about it. His views about the relative merits and obligations of the rich and the poor were peculiar, and very well defined. They could by no possibility have been brought into line with those of the Soviet Republic.

Moscow is no place for the Fairchild family.

I make a determined search for volume one, and can't find it—no one in the shop knows anything about it. Then "Mary" *did* take it to England.

And I shall take the other two volumes there.

The shopkeeper says that he has newer English books. He shows me a row of very old Tauchnitz volumes, various standard novels in good bindings —the private library of some Graf again?—a few American books of the 'nineties and nineteen-hundreds.

They can stay where they are.

They are not, like the Fairchild family, a part of English life and the English tradition. I pay a few roubles, take my two volumes—and the Fair-

child family, after all these years, has started its
journey home again.

CONVERSATION IN ROSTOV

I REACH ROSTOV AT MIDDAY AFTER A very hot, long journey and after a strange interlude of time spent on a Communal Farm.

It is like coming back to the world after being immured in a Trappist monastery.

The hotel personnel recognizes me—slightly to my surprise, for I feel exactly like Rip van Winkle —and after one look suggests that I should have a bath.

Either I am even dirtier than I supposed, or the Rostov Hotel is the most civilized spot in Russia, for this has never been proposed to me anywhere else.

I accept thankfully, and care not at all when earwigs share the bath with me and the towel turns out to be full of holes.

Afterwards my luggage—left behind, whilst I explored farm-life—is returned to me, and I find clean clothes (as opposed to clothes that have been repeatedly washed in a small bucket by myself) and put them on. As for the other things in the suitcase, they seem like relics of another age. The little saucepan, and the Meta fuel, bought at a

London shop . . . and the blue knitted jumper that I *didn't* sell to the lady in Moscow who clamoured to buy it . . . and the books . . . and good heavens! I'd forgotten all about that unopened pot of face-cream! Not that all the face-cream in the world can really restore to me an appearance of civilization. Only weeks of treatment and the combined efforts of the Beauty Parlour and the hairdresser can hope to do that, and none of it will be obtainable in Russia.

Still, I now look clean.

If only my letters from home were here—but they are all waiting for me at the Intourist bureau in Odessa.

Mrs. Trollope, to whom my thoughts have reverted so very, very often in the last long weeks, no doubt received news from England with the utmost irregularity, and when it did come, it was probably always unsatisfactory. Bailiffs in the house, and the children ill, and Mr. Trollope asking maddeningly hopeful questions about America, and more bailiffs. . . .

Mrs. Trollope survived it all, including the gigantic failure of her gigantic bazaar, and came home again, and got rid of the bailiffs, and wrote a best-seller.

My first meal in Rostov seems incredibly good and incredibly plentiful. Why did I ever think that Soviet catering was inadequate?

And how very gay the orchestra sounds, crashing its way full-speed through the old familiar tune: "Sous les Toits de Paris." I know just where the pianist and the violin will temporarily part company and then join up again—and so they do.

The visitors, of course, are all new. This seems to me natural. (I forget if Rip van Winkle skipped one generation, or two?)

At one table is a very old lady, who oughtn't to be travelling about Russia at all but sitting on the front at Bournemouth with a Pekingese at her feet —and a middle-aged man who addresses her as "moother."

There are several Russians, mostly men, and a party of French people who are celebrating something with kvass and carnations on the table—and a young woman with a pallid little boy who has sores on his little shaven head and a solemn expression.

Then I suddenly notice a solitary Englishwoman, whom I have surely seen before.

I VISIT THE SOVIETS

She is the lecturer on economics who has a travelling scholarship. . . . We met in Moscow.

After lunch I go up and greet her with such enthusiasm that she looks quite taken aback. She little knows that she seems, to me, as Stanley to Livingstone.

A not unfamiliar conversation ensues.

"I think we met in Moscow."

"I've been to Tiflis and the Caucasus. Have you done that?"

"No, I haven't. I'm going on to Odessa and home from there, first going by sea to Constantinople."

"How interesting, a friend of mine did that. She says the Roumanian boats are the best. I'm going out through Poland."

"That ought to be interesting."

It is a point of honour to suggest that whatever exit route is chosen, it is bound to be a very interesting one.

"Are you staying long in Rostov?"

"Only two days. Are you?"

"No, I leave for Warsaw on Thurs—I mean on the seventeenth."

We exchange rather a startled look, at the lapse

from propriety which has so nearly overtaken the conversation. In Russia there are no days of the week, and it has become indelicate to refer to them by name.

The lecturer on economics is, I find, to be taken to see a state farm on the following morning, and I decide to join in the excursion.

But in the night it rains.

Rostov, which is a cheerful, Southern-looking town, with semi-tropical vegetation, is now deluged and streaming. The streets are flooded, and all the drain-pipes overflow, and all the gutters, and still the heavens come down in torrents. (Not that they are the heavens, of course, over Russia. Merely the skies.)

The visit to the state farm has become impossible, owing to the condition of the road.

The question now arises, how does one spend a pouring wet sixteen hours in an hotel in Soviet Russia?

There are not even enough chairs to go round.

However, I establish myself early in one of the few that do exist, in the recess on the landing, and there read *David Copperfield*.

How well Dickens stands by one!

I VISIT THE SOVIETS

Of the half-dozen books I brought with me, three were by Dickens, and I wish now that all six had been.

The Mill on the Floss was good, especially the first half, but I like Maggie less and less as she grows older, and Stephen I like not at all. Nor do I know why I brought a book of which I am never able to read the end without tears.

The Cloister and the Hearth did me moderately well—but only moderately, and the manse at Gouda seems to me a most unsatisfactory climax. So it did, to do him justice, to the author.

As for Shakespeare, whom I took with me almost entirely because it seemed the proper thing to do, I am sure that we get on much better when I can *hear* the plays being acted on the stage. I read him in little patches and try and find out how many of the more famous speeches I can still repeat from memory, and learn one or two of the songs and sonnets. And there it ends.

I hope I am not like King George IV—but I dare say I am—though I doubt if I should have the moral courage to speak as plainly as he did.

Into these literary musings breaks the lecturer on economics.

I VISIT THE SOVIETS

Her state is a much worse one than mine, because to visit the farm was one of her main objects in coming to Rostov, and moreover she has no book at all and adds piteously that once she had some oranges but they are all finished now.

I can only offer her *The Mill on the Floss*—which I do—and in return borrow a pair of nail-scissors, as the pair I brought from England has been a failure throughout, and no nail-scissors can be obtained anywhere at all in the Soviet Union. (This is the considered utterance of all the Russians whom I consult.)

We do not, however, produce these objects of exchange on the instant. To do so would be to abandon the chairs—not to be thought of. Already a very large Russian Comrade with her head in a handkerchief, a French couple, and a man carrying a copy of *Pravda* and a portfolio have looked into the recess and angrily departed on seeing it occupied.

The recess is like the sodality of the Soviet Government—if you once drop out, you can never get back again.

We agree to collect the nail-scissors and *The Mill on the Floss* later in the day.

In the meantime, we talk.

The conversation is one of those singular and detached ones that are peculiar to strangers meeting in Russia.

"Have you been to see any of the Workers' Dwellings here?"

"Yes. They took me the first day. Some of the flats weren't bad. There was one two-roomed one though, where some people were living, and I only saw one bed."

"They say they have folding-beds, but I don't see where they can keep them."

"There isn't any privacy at all in Russia, is there?"

"None whatever. When I went over the Gynae-cological Clinic they took me *everywhere*. There wasn't so much as a screen."

"There never is."

"There was a man there, talking to one of the doctors. The guide stayed and listened for a few minutes and then told us that he was being given advice for venereal disease."

"How very agreeable. When we went to Bol-shevo — the prison colony near Moscow — the guide asked a good many of the prisoners what

[209]

their misdeeds had been, in order to tell us about them. I'm bound to say they always seemed quite ready to answer. One of the few times I've ever seen Russians laugh, is when they tell one about the activities that have landed them in Bolshevo. I suppose it's a good thing, to eliminate shame."

"I suppose so. I liked Bolshevo, and thought it an excellent system for young offenders. Self-discipline, and freedom, and work—and no separation amongst families, as they all live there together."

"Political prisoners don't get treated like that," says the lecturer very thoughtfully.

"No, I'm afraid not."

"They just disappear, or go to Siberia, or to work on the reconstructions somewhere."

And we tell one another stories, obtained at second- or third-hand, of persons who uttered unguarded expressions of opinion, behind locked doors and closed windows, concerning Comrade Stalin, or the Abortion Law, or the Constitution, and then walked out into the street and were never heard of more. And of Russian wives married to foreign husbands living in Paris or Geneva or Istanbul, writing indiscreet letters to relatives left behind in Moscow and one day vanishing abruptly and for ever from the country of their adoption.

"There's one thing," declares the lecturer with abrupt emphasis, "I shan't care if I never set eyes on a picture of Lenin or of Stalin again, as long as I live."

"Nor I. It seems very odd that in so large a country they should apparently only have two pictures, and should plaster them on every wall of every building, public or private."

"There are, on the whole, more of Lenin than of Stalin."

"He has a better face."

"Yes, that's true. Besides, there's more variety in the Lenin pictures. There's the one of him when he was three."

"Holding up two fingers, like a sort of infant Pope blessing the faithful."

"And in *exactly* the attitude of those Italian pictures of the Bambino. Mark my words," says the lecturer very impressively indeed, "the Bolsheviks are simply reverting to the old beliefs, in a new form. They're evolving a divinity, and his name is Lenin. Look at that Mausoleum, and the embalming, and all the relics in the museum, and every-

[211]

thing. And plenty of people are writing about him, and the peasants already have folk-songs about him. In twenty years' time I don't mind betting that all Soviet Russia will believe devoutly in the Virgin Birth of Lenin."

I think it extremely likely that she is right.

Then we talk about the thoroughgoing and determined way in which organized religion has been stamped out in the U.S.S.R., and organized physical culture, organized fun in public parks, and organized patriotism has been substituted instead.

I remember one or two of the funeral processions that I saw in Moscow.

A coffin, covered with a red flag, and a very few people walking forlornly behind it, and sometimes a feeble rendering of the "Internationale." And then, I suppose, cremation, and the official assurance that this life is all.

"Perhaps the young people like it all very much," I say doubtfully.

"Probably they do, as they are taught how fortunate they are from the time they can first breathe," says the lecturer rather caustically.

"Besides, they've never been in any other country but this one, and they never, I imagine, will be."

I ponder in silence the fate—that to me seems so unenviable—of the young people of the Soviet.

Presently we find that the rain is now only coming down violently instead of very violently, and that in the streets one or two people are racing and splashing along without umbrellas. Umbrellas, like nail-scissors, are not to be found in Russia, and this must be particularly hard on the inhabitants of a town in which it rains as it does in Rostov.

"Shall we make a dash for the cinema? Unless you would lend me a book," suggests the lecturer. "Do you know anything about a film called *Circus?*"

"Yes, I do. I saw it in Moscow."

It is a spirited, if involved, picture concerning a blonde circus-rider who gives birth in America to a baby which is under the double handicap— from the bourgeois point-of-view—of being both illegitimate and as black as a coal.

The story concerns the vicissitudes of this unhappy pair, who are pursued by a capitalist, in a top-hat and moustache, even into the very circus-ring itself. They escape into Soviet Russia, the top-hat is foiled, and the Russian circus patrons, en *bloc*, fall affectionately upon the black baby, hushing it until I am reminded of the infant Paul Dombey—"petted and patted till it wished its friends further." The scene closes in, as usual, with the singing of the "Internationale."

When I have given my résumé to the lecturer on economics, she decides at once that she prefers *The Mill on the Floss*.

WITHOUT COMMENT

THE SOVIET, BESIDES DISPENSING with the days of the week, dispenses also with God.

Thorough in this as in everything, it does not say: We will do without God and the days of the week, let others do as they will. It says: There is no God, there are no days of the week.

This is reiterated, with smiling firmness, by such authoritative people as the Intourist guides, the heads of various clinics and departments visited by tourists, and a number of very little Comrades who are interrogated on the subject by an enterprising German Professor when he and I visit a Kindergarten in Rostov.

"Ask these children," he demands of the guide, "whether they know anything about the good God."

The guide looks taken aback and so, for that matter, do I. Nobody else has ever made this vital enquiry so boldly.

"No, they do not."

"'But ask them, please."

The guide, rather sulkily, says in Russian that the Comrade from Germany wishes to know whether the children have ever heard the stories that the children of capitalist countries are obliged to read, out of the Bible—which is, I suppose, the nearest translation she can bring herself to make of so outrageous a question. The little Comrades all shake their heads and laugh merrily.

"We have no superstitious teaching in our schools," says the guide, choosing her words with a remarkable disregard for the feelings of other people.

I think the German, who is both earnest and talkative, is about to deliver a terrific argument, and in order to stop him I speak to the guide myself.

"We quite understand that no religious teaching is given in the schools—but what about their homes?"

The guide shrugs her shoulders.

"Their parents are free, if they wish, to tell them anything they like."

"And do they?"

"No. They are too enlightened. Only the elder generation, the grandparents, are sometimes too old to change."

"Supposing, though, that a child happened to

[216]

have religious parents, and was taught at home to say its prayers, and believe in God—what would happen?"

"He would come to school, and find that all the other children laughed at such things, and every day he would be taught that there is no God and religion is all superstition—and very soon he would just think that his parents were rather stupid people."

The guide, for the moment, has got the last word. What she has just said is so logical and reasonable that it can hardly fail to be true.

The German Professor makes a sound—something between a bark and a groan and tells me aside, in guttural French, that he would like to interrogate each child individually and in private.

I point out to him that this would be quite impossible in the time at his disposal—he is leaving Rostov tonight—and that in any case, the average age of these infidel Comrades being five years, he would get little of value from them.

"But I wish to study this question. It is for this that I have come to Russia."

What a heart-breaking mission!

"This afternoon we are visiting a school for

much older children—girls up to eighteen. Perhaps you could ask them some questions."

The guide, I know, will be anything but pleased. She is not nearly as nice as most of the guides I have had in Russia, or as any of the other Rostov guides.

She is a blonde with black eyebrows, and it is a very moot point whether the hair was dyed to contrast with the eyebrows, or the other way round, and what, in either case, made her think it a good idea. The resultant effect is an extraordinary combination of the sordid and the sinister.

"You will to the other school this afternoon with me come?" says the German, suddenly reverting to English.

Yes, I will.

I rather want to see the school on my own account, and I particularly wish to hear the valiant German plumbing this question of religion. All the tourists I have come across in Russia—and myself as well—have been thoroughly chicken-hearted about it. Amongst ourselves we have said:

"They've quite done away with religion."

"It's a pity about the churches."

"I may not go to Church very often myself, but

I must say, I don't like the thought of children being brought up as little heathens."

We none of us like the thought.

But we have all been either too shy, too anxious to seem broad-minded, or too determined to live and let live, to voice our dislike.

It is left to the German Professor to do it, and to me to witness his deed of valour.

I wish it were the nice little guide instead of the disagreeable one, who was coming with us. But this question of guides and tourists is one of the results of the Tower of Babel—as we say in Capitalist and Bible-reading countries.

The German Professor and I can both speak French, but his English is very bad and my German non-existent. Therefore we must be handed over to the guide who speaks French—the disagreeable one—while the nice guide who speaks English takes a party of Americans, and also Miss Blake and Miss Bolton, to inspect a pasteurized-milk factory.

The school to which the Professor and I are conducted is less democratic than it ought to be, in Soviet Russia. I am not clear about its exact status—whether it is a secondary school, or a technical school, or some more specialized establishment—but the pupils are not of peasant origin. They are the children of professional people.

The Headmaster is a tall, pallid, attenuated Russian. He doesn't stand a chance against the Professor, who explains five times very loudly and carefully in French that he wishes to talk with some of the scholars.

They are busy, says the Headmaster faintly.

We can wait, returns the Professor.

They can speak only Russian.

The guide is here to translate.

At this the guide breaks in and says something very rapidly in Russian. I think it is to the effect that the Comrade from Germany is a man of immense determination and that it will be simpler and speedier to let him have his way.

In fact, the Professor has already sat down, with an air of being rooted to the spot, that bodes ill for any hope of dislodging him.

The Headmaster gives in without a struggle and the first class is sent for—a dozen young girls, aged between fourteen and eighteen, and all of them reasonably alert and intelligent-looking.

It turns out that most of them understand French, and the eldest one speaks it. Throughout

[220]

the dialogue between her and the Professor, I take notes.

"You learn languages at school?"

"Yes, we are learning French and English."

"Can you speak English?"

"I can only read and write it a little, at present."

"You must learn to speak it. What do you wish to do, when you leave school?"

"Become a doctor."

The Professor asks this question, through the interpreter, of each girl. The replies vary very little.

"A doctor."—"An architect."—"An engineer." —And one or two "A pedagogue."

The Headmaster, perhaps thinking that I am feeling neglected, or perhaps in order to remind us that he is, after all, the Headmaster of the school and entitled to conduct the proceedings, enquires whether I wish to ask anything.

"Yes. Do they learn plain sewing, or cooking, at school?"

"No."

"Do any of them do either, at home?"

"One girl does needlework and likes it. None of them cook."

"What will they do when they leave, and take

[221]

up their professions?"

"They will eat in communal kitchens, so as to be free to pursue their work."

"Then somebody else will have to do the cooking? Even in a communal kitchen the meals won't prepare themselves."

"It will be arranged for them," says the guide evasively.

It will be arranged for them—and I can see exactly how. There will be a section of the community doing domestic labour in order to set another section free for work requiring a higher type of education.

A retrogression seems indicated, from the Soviet system of absolute equality for all.

The Professor, though listening civilly to my enquiries and at intervals nodding violently to show that he is following them, is obviously burning to begin again.

In his halting French he resumes his dialogue with the head girl.

"Do any of you ever go to Church?"

There is a second's stupefied silence. The girls look at one another—and then they suddenly all break out, quite spontaneously, into young, merry laughter.

"They are amused," says the guide, super-fluously.

The head girl turns to the Professor, still smiling. She is rather nice-looking—dark, and well-developed, with bright brown eyes and thick, curly hair.

"We know," she explains politely, "that the churches teach only superstition, and we cannot help laughing at the thought that we should waste our time in thinking about such things."

"What do your parents say?"

"They, also, know that it is superstition. It is only for the very old people, the grandparents. But we are the lucky Children of the Revolution."

The last phrase is a quotation. I have heard it sung by the children in the crèches and the clinics, time and again.

"Have you ever, any of you, read the Bible?"

"No. It would be of no use to us."

"How can you tell that, if you've never read it?"

"We know that it is none of it true. What is false, cannot be good."

"It has historical value. It has influenced the world for many hundreds of years."

"It has influenced it badly. We wish to forget all that, and make a new world, founded on reason and without superstition."

How well she has been primed—and how confident she is—and how young.

None of the others have read the Bible, either. They have never been inside a church. They have never said a prayer.

"Look at all the bad things that have been done in the name of this religion," says one child of about sixteen, very earnestly. "We have overthrown all that. We are no longer intolerant."

"But is it not intolerant to have sent away all the priests, and shut up or pulled down all the churches, so that people who want them cannot have them?"

"But," cries the head girl, "it is only a few old people who still want them! None of us do—none of the young!"

She has, I think, very neatly epitomized the new outlook.

Then the girls, feeling, I suppose, that they have disposed very thoroughly of the whole question of religion, ask whether in England girls and boys still learn the Scriptures.

"Certainly. It is an important part of the history of the world, and very beautiful literature besides."

"Do they also read the works of Darwin?"

"Those who wish to do so, no doubt."

"Then how," demands the head girl rhetorically, "can they believe in what the Bible says, if they have learned about the theory of evolution?"

She looks so pleased and triumphant, and so certain of having scored, that the Professor and I, quite involuntarily, I think, look at one another and smile.

I suggest—though without much hope of being taken seriously—that so mighty a subject has not escaped the attention of experts, and might properly be left to them.

But the young Comrades think that they themselves are experts—especially the head girl.

"In England," says the child, "you have evidently not studied Darwin."

"We not only study him, it was we who produced him in the first place."

It is not really a very sound retort, but it will do to close the subject.

The girls ask one other question.

[225]

"Is the ring that the English Comrade is wearing, a wedding-ring?"

Yes.

"In Russia, women do not wear wedding-rings any more. It is a badge of slavery."

In England, I assure them, it is not a badge of slavery. I point out to them that I have a profession of my own, that I travel to Russia or anywhere else when I wish to, and that I have as much freedom as any woman could possibly desire.

They do not believe one word of it.

They know better.

A marriage under God, says the head girl sapiently, is no better than slavery for the woman.

By the strange expression "under God" — in whose existence she does not believe—she means, evidently, "in a church."

I do not prolong the discussion.

The Professor, I think, would like to deliver a very earnest homily, but the guide and I—for once at one—unite in dissuading him.

The Russian Headmaster has had more than enough of us and our questions, and the girls can really add very little to what they have already said so plainly and with such ardent, innocent conviction.

The German and I make our farewells, thank
everybody with the one Russian word we all know
—"Spazeba"—and take our way back to the hotel
in silence.

Only when we have got rid of the guide, do we
speak.

"The Soviet methods — how thorough!" says
the Professor, casting up his hands and eyes.

Thorough, indeed.

"It is rather odd," I say, "that listening to those
girls should have reminded one of the Jesuits."

"The Jesuits?"

"Don't you remember: 'Give me a child until it
is seven years old . . .'?"

SAVOYARD

(1)

"WHO IS THIS PERSON THAT YOU'VE taken up with?" says the lecturer on economics into my ear.

I think that she has worded her enquiry offensively, and reply in a distant way that he is a French agronome. I hope she knows better than I do exactly what this means.

He is also a Savoyard. He has just told me so. Why do I at once remember something about a poem that I used to recite at the age of about eight —"Le Petit Savoyard": "Pars, pauvre enfant, cheche ton pain——" and each verse ended up, very sadly, with: "Adieu, la patrie!"

If I could remember solid pieces of information with the same readiness with which I can remember irrelevant snatches of bad verse, I also, might be an agronome by this time—or perhaps even a lecturer on economics. As it is, I am one of a group of tourists being taken by two guides to look at a Collective Farm not far from Rostov. I have got myself mixed up with the French Group, by mistake, and have to hear all about the number of cows, the method of pig-feeding and the exact rights of the Collective farm-holders, in French.

(In another room, I am told afterwards, the lecturer on economics electrifies everybody by knowing the Russian for manure. This lends a touch of distinction to the English group for the rest of the day.)

The Savoyard speaks no language but his own —and in that, he speaks almost without ceasing. Whilst we are walking round the cow-houses he asks me, in a low voice, if I think that the guides *really* translate all our questions accurately?

Yes, I do.

He is relieved, but not wholly convinced.

"On nous cache sûrement quelque chose."

This, I find out later, is an obsession with him. He has come to obtain information about Russia, for his village, and feels that it is being withheld.

What information?

Every information, he replies largely. But perhaps especially prices. Can I tell him anything about prices?

I can, and do, tell him that I paid the equivalent of two shillings and sixpence for two apples, in

Leningrad. He whips out a little book in which to write this down, but is stumped by the two shillings and sixpence, and we have to work it out, slowly, in francs and then in roubles.

We are shown a vineyard, in excellent condition, and of an immense number of acres. Nobody says anything very intelligent about this. I think my own effort is the best—and all I ask is whether they ever get any disease amongst the vines? If they say Yes I can nod, as if I'd thought as much, and if they say No that will be a satisfaction to them in itself.

They say: Sometimes.

But not this year, I suggest confidently.

Not this year. Not at present.

No, I thought not.

We see farm buildings, and the usual crèche for the children of the workers, and the children themselves — very sturdy and brown, and all dressed in little mauve cotton shorts and nothing else. They sing a Revolutionary Song, very gaily and quite out of tune, and then all run off to a meal, with Stalin on the wall as presiding deity. He has a red bow on the corner of his frame—like a kitten on a chocolate-box.

[230]

I VISIT THE SOVIETS

Miss Blake and Miss Bolton wish to see inside the homes of some of the farm workers. Is this possible?

Yes, it is.

This is the first farm they have visited, and they don't know—as the economic lecturer and I do—that it is almost always possible to visit one of the houses.

The Savoyard apparently does know, because he points to a very small dwelling—one of the smallest, and most out-of-the-way — and suggests that we should visit that one.

No, that is not possible. At that house today they are all busy. It must be another house, a much bigger and more prosperous-looking one, chosen by the man who is showing us round, and heavily recommended by the guide.

"Vous voyez bien! On nous cache quelque chose."

And the Savoyard declines to take any interest in the house, where there are two rooms for one family of mother and two daughters, and the furniture is nice and new-looking, and everything very clean.

In a sense he is right. It is not in the least a

typical workers' dwelling, as I very well know from personal experience—but on the other hand, is it reasonable to object to that?

Naturally we, the foreigners, are taken to the show places. Naturally, the best is brought forward for inspection and the less good left in the background.

The farm itself is a show farm, one of the best of the Collective Farms. Some day they may all be like this, but at present they are not. In the meantime, visitors are taken to see the successes, and not the failures — and I think exactly the same procedure would obtain in any other country in the world, just as much as in Russia.

All this I expound to the Savoyard, whilst we walk through cherry orchards. He listens politely and at the end of it all he replies:

"Oui, oui. Mais tout de même — on a l'air de nous cacher quelque chose."

In spite of it all he is cheerful, and says Allons, en avant! and springs about when most of the rest of us are wilting from heat and fatigue. He has two compatriots—one of them a young and giggling Frenchwoman who says she is a *pédagogue de psychologie* and has come to Russia to study the

law about abortion. (Why?) The other is a young
man who speak~ not at all, and of whom the
Savoyard mutters to me between his teeth: "Il est
Israelite."

Neither of his compatriots attracts him, evidently. This makes it more understandable,
though less flattering, when he invites me to the
seat beside him for the drive back to Rostov, and
tells me all about his impressions of Russia—
which are bad. In fact he has so much to say
against the Soviet system, and says it with so much
and such violent prejudice, that I find myself
driven to defend it.

He does not listen.

On this basis we get on admirably. The Savoyard
talks, very fast and generally between clenched
teeth, so that it is extremely difficult to hear more
than one word in six, and I listen and say, "Mais
oui." Sometimes I add "Seulement"—but that is
as far as I ever get.

I think, perhaps, there is some justification for
the expression used by the economic lecturer.
Whether or not I've taken up with the Savoyard,
he has definitely taken up with me.

He comes and sits at my table for meals — and

meals that, in any other country, might be an affair of thirty-five minutes or so, here, in Russia, take an hour and a half. This enables him to get through a great deal of conversation.

Some of it is about Russia, and the system of concealment that he feels is being practised there, and a good deal of it is about prices — prices in France, in Russia, in England (which he has never visited) and in the United States (where he has never been). I am a great success when I tell him that, in England, a tax has been put upon tea.

He writes it down in his little book.

At the next table are his compatriots — with whom he ought to be sitting. The female *pédagogue* who is evidently very single-minded, can be heard pursuing her subject at intervals:

"Mais après le quatrième mois, non . . .

"Jamais plus de trois fois dans une même année . . . j'ai demandé . . ."

I am sure that she asked. I am sure that she carried her enquiries to the ultimate limits of decency, and beyond them. In Soviet Russia, one publicly asks questions and receives replies on subjects that in other countries are reserved for the consulting-room. Were not Peter and I, in

Moscow, shown a large chair, that I quite mistook for a dental chair, until informed of its real nature—which was of a sinister description that must have delighted the *pédagogue de psychologie* when she saw it—as I'm certain she did.

Her vis-à-vis, the Israelite, speaks hardly at all. When he does, he sounds wretched.

The Savoyard says that, in addition to being an Israelite, he is also a French Communist. He tells me about how he—the Savoyard—once defeated a French Communist at a municipal election and how, after the defeat, the very dogs of the town turned their heads away when the Communist went by.

I think this is very dramatic, and reflects well upon the dogs' intelligence, if not upon their kindness of heart.

Presently the Savoyard suggests that I should go with him to Yalta, Sevastopol and the Crimea generally, in two days' time.

No, it is most amiable of him to suggest it, but I am obliged to go to Odessa.

In what way am I *obliged* to go there?

The true answer to this is, in no way at all. I just feel that I would rather go to Odessa by myself than to the Crimea with a strange agronome.

I utter something mysterious to the effect that I must, at all costs, pick up my English letters in Odessa, and hope he will think they are of international importance, involving the gravest transactions.

Fortunately he is, as usual, paying no attention to my words. I don't think he takes them in at all, until later in the day, when he suddenly informs me that from Odessa we shall get a particularly good view of a solar eclipse expected in a few days' time.

We?

Yes, he will be in Odessa then. After finishing with Yalta, Sevastopol and the Crimea he is coming by boat to Odessa.

"On s'y retrouvera," he says—not sentimentally, but with cheerful confidence.

In the meanwhile he has asked to be taken to another, special, farm tomorrow, and he hopes that I will come too.

The alternatives are a bread factory and a Museum of the Revolution.

I choose the farm.

The bread factory I may perhaps see later—but

[236]

not the Museum of the Revolution, if I can help it. I saw one in Leningrad, and one in Moscow, and one somewhere else. The Museum of Propaganda would be a much better name for them, and it is a crude form of propaganda, at that.

There are frightful highly-coloured pictures of peasants undergoing various forms of torture, and of bloated capitalists drinking champagne and embracing hideous women, and there are Madame-Tussaud-like little groups of soldiers in the snow shooting revolutionaries in the snow, and a great deal of red paint splashed about everywhere.

Some of the documents would probably be very interesting if I could understand them, and I have no doubt that a good many of the exhibits are really worth having. But the more strikingly obvious ones are only disagreeable, without being convincing. An exception is the photographic record of many of the events of October 1917, which is of course of real historical value.

Busts, statues and pictures of Lenin fill up every gap. He is everywhere: exhorting, urging, threatening—the Capitalists—getting in and out of trains that are taking him to or from exile, and sitting writing in a little den in Finland.

[237]

In one of the museums was a letter from a Department in London, setting forth reasons why Lenin should not receive a transit-visa through Great Britain. "A capable organizer and highly intelligent . . . a most dangerous man."

One would like to know exactly how that letter found its way to Russia.

(2)

The special farm is to be visited, by the Savoyard and myself, at 11 o'clock in the morning.

When Intourist says 11 o'clock—and sometimes adds, colloquially, the word "sharp"—it is safe to assume that the expedition really will be taking place at about 11.45 or very soon after.

The Savoyard, however, is ready by 11, and sitting in Intourist's office. I look in on him once or twice, just to show that I am pleased and excited and looking forward to it all, and then go into the hall to say goodbye to Miss Blake and Miss Bolton who are leaving us, on their way home to England.

Their train goes at 1 o'clock and they have been told to be ready at 11—"sharp."

I hear myself asking all the customary questions.

[238]

"Are you travelling 'hard' class?"

"Yes. We're used to it now, and it's the last time. Besides, one gets more air that way."

"So one does. Will there be any food on the train?"

"No one seems to know. They're giving us some food to take with us."

"I suppose it'll be the same as usual: brown bread and cheese and *that* sausage, and a bottle of mineral water?"

"I expect so. Well, it's been very interesting."

"Oh yes, it's been most interesting."

"Thoroughly interesting."

"Nobody seems able to tell us what time our train arrives tomorrow morning."

"When I came here, the journey took thirty-six hours. But we were late."

"Yes, I expect so."

"Well — goodbye, Miss Blake. Goodbye, Miss Bolton. I hope you'll have a good journey."

Everybody echoes these sentiments and Miss Blake and Miss Bolton make suitable acknowledgments.

A guide—for whom everybody has been waiting for nearly an hour — comes up and says rather reproachfully:

"You are ready? Then come, please."

They all, except Miss Blake and Miss Bolton, depart for the bread factory and I go to the office to rejoin the Savoyard.

The moment I enter it I become aware that the atmosphere is electric.

The whole of the Intourist personnel is sitting about, looking harassed beyond description, and the agronome—in a towering rage—is planted on a chair in the middle of the rooms and looks as though he might have apoplexy at any moment. They have just told him that the special farm cannot, after all, be visited.

They are all busy there today.

They are sick.

The roads are not good.

They do not answer the telephone.

It is going to rain.

If only they stuck to *one* excuse—but that they never do. No person or institution is ever just sick, or busy, or unable to receive one. They are all three things, at one and the same time.

No wonder the Savoyard says, in a fury, that he is being deceived—things are being hidden from

The agronome—in a towering rage—is planted on a chair in the middle of the rooms.

him—they are afraid of what he may find out.

"Demain, peutêtre," feebly says Intourist.

(He is going away tonight, as we all know.)

I am sorry for the Savoyard, I am sorry for the Intourist personnel.

"Monsieur, calmez-vous je vous en supplie."

"Non madame. Je ne me calmerai pas."

What can one do, if he deliberately determines that he will *not* calm himself?

Nor does he.

On the contrary.

They offer him the bread factory, the Park of Rest and Culture, the Museum of the Revolution and a Lying-in Hospital.

He will have nothing to do with any of them. Either he sees the farm, or nothing.

"They cannot receive us."

In another minute, Intourist is going to tell us all over again that they are all busy, sick, and unable to answer their telephone.

In order to avert this I madly suggest to the Savoyard that he and I should take the tram and catch up the bread-factory expedition.

"Comme ça, on apprendra le prix de la farine."

He is quite unmoved.

A sort of lull falls, and we all look at one another.

How unfortunate it is that these contretemps should occur. Personally, I imagine that the farms, factories, clinics, crèches and various other institutions in Russia periodically revolt against having their day's work interrupted by sight-seers—and I don't blame them.

But I wish Intourist could evolve a more effective attitude about it. The fact is that they are not accustomed to strong-minded tourists. Most of us submit, without very much fuss, when told that the person or the institution we particularly wish to see will have nothing whatever to do with us.

"Alors, monsieur, vous ne voulez pas m'accompagner à la panification?"

"Non madame," he says, with a straightforward simplicity that Intourist might do well to imitate.

"Mais qu'allez-vous faire?"

"Je reste ici. Ou je vais à la ferme, ou je reste ici. Je ne bouge pas."

He no longer rages. He is become like Maud—icily regular, splendidly null.

He definitely gives me the impression that he will stay where he is, if necessary, for ever.

I think Intourist also feel this. They look at one

another in a pale, startled way.

At last the one who is in charge of the others—I think they call her the Head Lady—says something in Russian, and I hear the word "telephone." They are going to try again.

Knowing that this will take a very long while indeed, and seeing that the Savoyard has relaxed no iota of his Medusa-like fury, I decide *not* to sit down on another chair opposite him, or we should be too like the lady and gentleman who sat glaring at one another on two chairs like two mad bulls in the back drawing-room—"and there's the back drawing-room still at the back of the house to prove my words."

After *David Copperfield* and *Great Expectations*, I think I like *Little Dorritt* best of Dickens's novels, mostly on account of Flora and Mrs. F.'s Aunt.

I say thoughtfully to myself "There's milestones on the Dover Road," and walk out into the hall.

"We've not gone yet, you see."

Miss Blake and Miss Bolton, looking rather wan, are still with us.

"Oh dear. Well, I expect you've got plenty of time, really."

"We should have gone to the bread factory, if we'd known."

"Yes, of course. How tiresome they are. I hope they're giving you some food to take with you?"

"Yes. Brown bread, and cheese, and sausage and a bottle of mineral water."

Haven't we said all this before — or was it on some other occasion, with a different set of fellow-travellers?

"No one seems to know whether there'll be a dining-car on the train or not."

"Oh dear."

"They can't even tell us what time we shall get there, tomorrow morning."

"Oh dear, oh *dear! How* tiresome they are! Well, I do hope you'll be all right. Goodbye again. I hope you'll have a good journey."

"Goodbye."

I haven't really got anywhere to go, and might just as well stay in the hall, but that I can't think of anything in the least new or interesting to say in order to pass the time for Miss Blake and Miss Bolton.

Better walk up the stairs to the little recess where I sometimes sit when its solitary chair is unoccupied. Russian hotels have no place in which one can, officially, sit—except the entrance-hall. And neither in the hall nor anywhere else are there ever enough chairs.

No luck in the recess. A monumental Russian in a blouse is sitting there, holding his shaven head in both his hands as if it might at any minute come off.

When he sees me he asks me the time. Russians are always asking one the time, like idle small boys in London.

They do it, I think, because they themselves usually have no watch, and feel they may as well take advantage of any watch that does happen to cross their path. The actual time itself is of no importance to them.

Often, after ascertaining the time, they go on looking at the watch in a hypnotized sort of way, just for the satisfaction of seeing it.

This one does so now.

Then he sighs heavily, and says something that I don't understand.

I say—in Russian—that I can't speak Russian. Can *he* speak English?

"Niet."

"French?"

"Niet."

Then he asks if I can speak German.

"Niet."

My last card is always to say "Italianski?"—but it never meets with any success, and doesn't now.

The Russian makes me a long, and I'm sure polite, speech—I think to the effect that if only we had any language in common, we could certainly have had a most interesting conversation.

I nod energetically and say "Da, da," I make a civil reference to the beauties of Rostov, and he seems to cheer up.

What a pity it is we can't converse!

We *do* converse.

We converse for quite a long time. I am astonished to find what a lot we manage to convey to one another. I should do even better if only he would stick to Russian, of which I do understand quite a number of words, instead of mixing it up with German of which I understand absolutely nothing except "Danke schön" and "Ich liebe dich"—neither of which he says.

He tells me that he works at a Technical Institue, that his home is in Odessa, that he has never

[246]

had time to get married because he has always worked so hard, and that he thinks London must be an interesting town.

In return I inform him that I, also, work — I write—that I am going to Odessa presently, that I have a husband and two children in England, and that London is a fine town but the air is black. (By this I mean that it is sometimes foggy, and I really put it in because "air" and "black" are two of the Russian words that I happen to know.)

Then we talk about books — which is much easier than it sounds, because we confine ourselves wholly to Russian authors with world-famous names, the titles of whose works it is very simple to identify. He says what good books they are, and I say Yes, yes, and add that they are much read and discussed in England, and then he says Yes, yes.

Then I boldly plunge into opera, and tell him that I heard *Eugene Onegin* in Moscow, but here I come to grief. Opera is, evidently, the Russian's long suit. He bursts into a spate of eloquence, and I am lost. Presently he perceives this, and reverts to German again.

I feel that the time has come for us to part.

His last speech to me contains, in tones of passionate regret, the word "Esperanto!"

Ah yes, indeed! Esperanto! If only——

Still, we have done better than I should have thought possible, even without Esperanto.

"Dos vidanyah."

"Dos vidanyah."

(3)

I can't pass Miss Blake and Miss Bolton again. It's impossible.

If I ignore them they will think me disagreeable and ill-mannered, and if I speak what on earth can I say except all the things that I've said twice already, and that everybody else has also said already?

However, impossible or not, I've got to do it. By no other means can I reach the Intourist office.

"Not gone yet, you see!"

"No? How very tiresome for you, to have to wait like this. Still, the train's sure to be late."

"We could have gone to the bread factory."

I make a sound indicative—I hope—of deep concern, and pass on.

I VISIT THE SOVIETS

In the office the scene has entirely altered.

The Savoyard has won.

Intourist, in a deep state of gloom, is sending a special guide to take him to inspect the Collective Farm. The Collective Farm has, apparently, recovered from its sickness, returned from its absence, and put its telephone into action again.

The agronome is as sunny as Intourist is the reverse. He tells me, not once, but many hundreds of times, that "Patience et longueur de temps, Font plus que force ni que rage." *Longueur de temps* has played its part, beyond a doubt, but I don't feel that it is for him to talk about *patience* in those triumphant tones.

We go to the farm in a tram—it is quite a short distance — and I succeed in getting a seat for the last twenty minutes, and am pleased—and quote to myself, quite involuntarily, "I have learned to be glad at last of a little thing"—and when we do get there, it seems to me very like the one we saw the other day, only perhaps not so grand.

The guide works like a black, as usual, translating all the questions shot at her by the Savoyard, and all the replies made, with great deliberation, by the Russian in the office.

We then, also as usual, inspect.

I am only present as the appendage of my agronome friend, so need not originate any intelligent observations on my own account, which is a relief. My only achievement is to notice that there are rats in the long shed where the pigs are stalled. I see them jump out of the troughs, and scuttle into dark corners, as we go by.

When I tell this to the agronome, quietly, he asks if I am certain that they were not mice?

I am absolutely certain, and not at all pleased at having it supposed that I don't know the difference between a mouse and a rat.

He writes the rats down in his little book.

On the way back, when the guide is out of earshot, I ask him whether he thinks the little book will occasion trouble at the Customs? Will the officials wish to detain it for inspection, before allowing it to leave Russia? But perhaps he means to carry it in his pocket.

He does—but unfortunately I have suggested a disastrous idea to him.

"Si on va me fouiller, par exemple!"

"Mais non, mais non!"

"Ah! il ne manquerait que cela! Me fouiller, par

exemple——!"

Why in the world did I ever put the idea into his head? It keeps him in a state of boiling indignation all the rest of the way.

If they do search him, at the Customs—which is in the highest degree improbable—he will have no indignation left to vent upon them, having worked it all off at the mere idea.

By the time we get back to the hotel he has been *fouillé'd* under circumstances of the utmost indignity—he has resisted to the last gasp—he has demanded, and obtained the instant intervention of the French Embassy — a public apology has been offered him, and received by him with an enormous, and slightly ungenerous, lecture on the shortcomings of the whole of the Soviet Republic —an international incident of the utmost gravity has barely been averted.

I precede him into the hotel feeling quite weak from the stress and strain of it all—and am made no better by once more coming face to face with Miss Blake and Miss Bolton—whom I have forgotten all about—sitting back-to-back on one chair.

"Tiens! Je les croyais parties!" says the Savoyard quite merrily.

How mercurial he is.

"Bolton is feeling rotten," says Miss Blake glumly.

I am not surprised to hear it.

"Qu'est-e qu'elle dit?"

"Elle dit que son amie est malade."

"Tiens!" says the Savoyard indifferently, and he walks away upstairs.

I stop to make enquiries. Either I have a kinder heart, or better manners, than he has. Or is it that I am lacking in a quality that in my convent-school days was called *la simplicité* and was held in high esteem?

"Can I do anything?"

"I don't think so, thank you. She just feels rotten."

"Perhaps it's the long wait. Are you—is it likely that you'll be starting for the station fairly soon?"

"Oh, they made a mistake about the time of the train. It doesn't leave till 4 o'clock."

"We could perfectly well have gone to the bread factory," says Miss Bolton in an enfeebled voice.

She certainly does look a very bad colour.

"Couldn't you lie down till it's time to start?"

"Somebody else has got our room."

I reluctantly, and from a sense of duty to a compatriot, offer mine and hope I don't look too obviously relieved when the offer is refused.

Then the bread-factory expedition comes in, and everybody, walking through the hall, looks with astonishment at Miss Blake and Miss Bolton, to whom everybody has said goodbye at least twice already.

"You haven't gone yet?"

"No, we haven't gone yet. There was a mistake about the time of the train."

"Oh dear!"

"We could perfectly well have done the bread factory, if only we'd known sooner."

"My friend isn't feeling too chippy," says Miss Blake in a worried manner.

"She oughn't to travel 'hard' class."

"She ought to lie down till it's time to start."

"She ought to find out if there's an English doctor anywhere. Though of course, that wouldn't be much good if you really are leaving."

"I think," says Miss Blake, "that what she needs is a little brandy. Only we haven't got any with us. Would it be safe to buy Russian brandy?"

[253]

Everybody is of opinion that it wouldn't be—I don't quite know why. Two or three people handsomely offer to fetch their own flasks, and after a great deal of demurring from Miss Bolton, a sort of round-robin of brandy is collected in the top of a thermos flask and she drinks it, and looks less green.

Miss Blake thanks everybody in a proprietorial manner and says that Me friend thinks it must be something she ate.

It is noticeable that nobody has enquired what her symptoms are.

We all know, only too well, having all—at one time or another—suffered from them ourselves.

The friends of all of us in England, I have ascertained in various conversations, said to us — "In Russia you will get diarrhoea. Everyone does. Try—

Burnt brandy.

Arrowroot.

Boiled milk if you can get it.

Bicarbonate of soda.

A special prescription I can lend you, given me by a Russian ballet-dancer before the war."

I VISIT THE SOVIETS

I am very, very sorry for Miss Bolton, who has to face a long journey in a Russian train, in which the toilet accommodation will be of a thoroughly discouraging description.

The Savoyard leaves Rostov before I do. But we are to meet again in Odessa, and witness the eclipse of the sun, and visit farms, and compare notes of all the prices that we have been able to investigate. When he has actually gone — after a good deal of excited chat about his luggage, his passport, and the time of his train—the lecturer on economics recognizes me once more. (During the Savoyard interlude, she has had nothing to say to me.)

"What did he write in the Visitors' book? Most people are so fulsome. I know he wrote something, because I saw him doing it."

"Let's look at it."

It is quite a brief entry, and rather pathetic.

"Pourquoi pas de vases de nuit—cependant bien nécessaires?"

I admit that I have often wondered the same thing. I suggest that it is hygienic, and labour-saving, to dispense with the *vases de nuit.*

"Oh, is it on principle?" says the lecturer on economics.

She adds very thoughtfully:

"I'd always supposed that they must all have got broken in the Revolution."

I have parted with the lecturer. She has gone to Poland. I am sorry to see her go, and have a recrudescence of feeling like *L'orpheline de Moscou.*

A fresh lot of tourists arrive — Swedes and Armenians—and I assume the character of Oldest Inhabitant of the hotel. This carries with it no *prestige:* I resent them, and they resent me. Intourist tells me, coldly, that I have seen everything there is to see in Rostov and it is going to rain.

They are quite right: it does rain. It rains so hard that nobody can do anything or go anywhere and the chairs in the hotel are at more of a premium than ever. The sight of an unoccupied seat in the recess on the landing is the signal for a kind of grim game of musical chairs with no music and only one chair.

Definitely, the time has come for me to go to Odessa. Like Miss Blake and Miss Bolton, I receive a white paper parcel containing bread, cheese, sausage and mineral water — like them, I am left planted in the hall for a long, indefinite period of time before a guide comes and takes me away and sees me into the train.

This time, I have paid a supplement and am travelling soft instead of hard, because I am tormented by an intermittent toothache that is never quite bad enough to keep me awake, but always feels as if it were just going to be.

How luxurious it is to be lying on a stuffed seat with a holland cover, instead of on a wooden plank! How extraordinarily fortunate I am to have the carriage all to myself!

I shall keep the bread, cheese and sausage for breakfast — by which time I may be sufficiently hungry to like the look of them — and half the mineral water. The other half I drink, reserving a little in which to wash my teeth.

My tooth — perhaps as a result of the mineral water?—doesn't ache and I go to sleep.

When I awake it is light, and within three feet of me a Red Army officer, his uniform neatly folded at his feet, lies placidly in the opposite bunk. He has been inserted there, without my knowledge, during the night.

I VISIT THE SOVIETS

He bows over the top of the sheet, and I bow in return.

He is evidently awake for good: so am I. Will he make a move to get up, or is he going to have the good feeling to turn his face to the wall?

I give him every opportunity: he doesn't take them. I turn my face to the wall and pretend to sleep, but nothing happens.

Then I remember that Russians, if a two-night journey is before them, very often spend the whole of the intervening day without getting up at all: merely sitting about in pyjamas on the unmade bed.

Of course, we *could* both do this. But on the whole I prefer the bolder course of getting out of bed, putting on my dressing-gown and slippers and marching off with most of my clothes to wait about in the corridor until I can get into a disengaged lavatory.

Theoretically, I think the Russian's attitude is the right and sensible one. In practice, I don't really much like it.

When I return, however, washed and clad, I find him fully dressed in his uniform. I do not know if he is washed or not.

I VISIT THE SOVIETS

Most of the day he sits looking out of the window—speechless. I sit in the corridor, where there are little flap-seats at intervals, and read *Our Mutual Friend* until I laugh so much over Mr. Wegg, and Mr. Venus soaking his powerful mind in tea, that I am obliged to leave off.

I should like to soak my own powerful mind in tea, too, but none is forthcoming.

Then two very young Russians—boys of about eighteen—come up and want to know what I am reading.

Dickens? Ah yes—but he had *bourgeois* ideals, they say, shaking their heads sadly.

I think it wise to turn the conversation onto Tolstoy, Maxim Gorki and Tchekov. One can never go wrong there, since one, naturally, praises these great names and does not presume to criticize.

But what extraordinary solidarity has been established amongst the Comrades — especially the young ones. All equally convinced that "there is only one god and what-you-may-call 'em is his prophet." Perhaps all the ones who don't subscribe to this are put away somewhere, out of sight? Certainly, one doesn't meet them.

(4)

The Savoyard is at Odessa before me. He hails me as I enter the hotel, and tells me that we are to watch the eclipse of the sun at 7 o'clock next morning. In the meanwhile, he has a table for me in the garden.

"C'est gentil."

Yes, it is. There is a little fountain, and some goldfish, and some very tall shady trees—much the nicest dining-room I have seen yet. It turns out, however, that the Savoyard has selected his table less with a view to the charms of its situation, than because he thinks it a favourable one for private conversation.

While we wait for our *bortsch* he leans forward and tells me, in a rapid, dramatic kind of way, between his clenched teeth, all about the places he has visited since we parted.

This *must* be what he is saying, because I catch the words "Sévastopol," "la Crimèe," and "On nous cachait sûrement la véritè, à Yalta." His conviction that he is being deceived is as strong as ever—stronger, I think.

I wish I could hear *all* that he is saying. What I

do hear is stirring to a degree.

"On est mieux dehors. Méfiez-vous des microphones!"

"Espions . . ."

Then a long, terrific mutter about something —I can't hear what—that happened to someone— impossible to distinguish who it was—who wrote an indiscreet letter and posted it in Moscow.

I roll my eyes suitably and ejaculate.

". . . les prisoniers . . . la Sibérie . . ."

"Oui, oui, oui."

"Vous comprenez, ils n'en parlent jamais."

"Naturellement."

How dramatic it all is. I wish I knew where he got all this spate of information, and how much of it is accurate—and I wish I didn't know him to be quite so violently prejudiced. How odd it is that everybody who comes to the Soviet Union is either insanely hostile, or insanely enthusiastic, about it. No golden mean. Perhaps I shall be its first impartial observer? Not if I listen much longer to my agronome, though.

His eyes starting from his forehead, he leans across the *bortsch* and hisses at me.

". . . dans le Kremlin . . . dans les mines . . .

dans le fleuve à Leningrad!"

When at last I leave him, to go and unpack, I feel quite worn out with vicarious agitation. I shall go to bed early—especially if I am to get up early and look at the eclipse tomorrow morning.

As a matter of fact I get up even earlier than I had wished or intended to, for the enthusiastic Savoyard rings up my bedroom just before 6 o'clock and urges me to come down at once.

We then wait for an hour on the front, overlooking the port, and are joined in course of time by some Germans, a couple of waiters from the hotel, and two old women with black shawls over their heads. Only the Germans, and one of the waiters, are interested in the eclipse. The Germans have pieces of smoked glass—which they politely hand round at intervals, like refreshments — and the Savoyard and I have dark spectacles.

Why isn't there a large crowd of intelligent scientists with telescopes, looking at this phenomenon? But perhaps they are all gathered together in some great observatory, in another part of the country.

Here, the eclipse isn't really total. The sun is greatly reduced, bit by bit, but a thin sliver remains, like a new moon.

For ten minutes we gaze upwards, blinking through black glass.

"Ca y est!" says the Savoyard at last, bringing the eclipse to a conclusion.

I find myself thanking him, as if he had arranged the whole thing, and he accepts my gratitude amiably.

We breakfast together, visit the town, the bathing-beach and the Museum together, lunch and dine together, and at 10 o'clock in the evening I am preparing to say goodbye to him in the hall. Then I discover that he trustfully supposes he is going to be able to change his remaining roubles into francs again.

I explain, as gently as I can, that such is never the practice of the Soviet Government. Long before I have finished, the cries of the Savoyard have brought round us nearly everybody in the hotel.

"Comment! On me laisse avec ces maudits roubles. . . !"

"Dépensez-les, monsieur," someone suggests. (Perhaps someone who has something to sell?)

"Donnez-les à un ami qui reste en Russie."

"Tell him," says an American tourist to me—

as being held responsible, I suppose, for the agronome and his *crise de nerfs*—"tell him that they'll take it all away from him at the Customs. They won't let any Russian money go out of the country."

I do tell the agronome this. Everybody else tells it him, in French, English and even Russian. It isn't that he hasn't understood the first time—he has, only too well—but his agitation is so frightful that we all feel obliged to say something, and really there isn't anything else *to* say.

At last someone has a new idea, and enquires how much money he actually has, unchanged?

Forty roubles and twenty-two kopeks.

Something under two pounds.

The American, doubtless accustomed to dealing with millions, loses all interest and walks away and only two Russians remain, to argue patiently. (Russians, I feel convinced, never walk away from any argument, even when — as in the present instance—it is conducted by persons to whom one another's languages are unintelligible.)

I also remain—partly from loyalty to my Savoyard, and partly because he and the Russians expect me to translate for them. This I do by inventing short, conciliatory speeches on the part of the Russians, and repeating them in French, and then saying in Russian "Yes, yes, he has understood"—which I can only hope will distract their attention from all that the agronome is really saying, and which requires no interpretation whatever.

At last Intourist brings it all to a close by announcing that it is time to go to the station. Sharp.

"Et vous ne voulez pas me changer mon argent?"

No, it is impossible.

Intourist has the face to add that he can give up his Russian currency at the Customs—where it will infallibly be taken from him in any case.

At this, I say in French — which I hope this particular guide understands—that it would be a great deal more satisfactory to spend it all on drink before he goes.

"N'ayez pas peur," says the Savoyard between his teeth. "J'aimerais mieux le brûler que de leur laisser."

I believe him.

Then, with his usual mercurial change of front, he clasps my hand, bows over it, kisses it and says gallantly: "Madame, mes hommages!"

We exchange cards—like two duellists—and say that we must meet again, which we well known to be most unlikely, and he departs.

And I say to myself, idiotically, as I go upstairs:

"Va, petit mousse,
Où le vent te pousse——"

SPECIAL INVESTIGATION

CONTINUALLY I HEAR MY FELLOW tourists being described by the guides, or by one another, or sometimes even by themselves, as specialists.

"Ah, she is a specialist in Agriculture. She has been sent here by her Association."

"He is a medical specialist. He wishes to inspect clinics."

"As a psychologist, I am interested in schools . . ."

"He is a historian. He likes Museums . . ."

"She is a Social Worker. She is to see the Home for Reformed Prostitutes at 2 o'clock sharp."

What can I say?

Sometimes the Intourist Bureau turns to me and asks me what my specialty is.

Can I tell them that an eminent American publisher has sent me to the Soviet because nobody has as yet tried to be funny about it? All along, I have said, weakly, that I am a journalist. Some people seem to have believed it: others not. One young woman, after closely inspecting the initials on my suitcase, told me at once that she felt sure I was

Miss Ethel M. Dell. We got on very well, and fortunately she never asked whether she was right or not. I suppose she felt too sure.

I should like to be a specialist also, but should be found out in a moment if I pretended to expert knowledge of factories, or crèches or farm tractors. Nor can I tell the truth and say that I am really most interested in human beings, because if I did everybody would become self-conscious—myself included.

(Besides, people who are interested in people rather than in things are much looked down upon, as I found out even in my nursery days. Only Pope ever thought well of them.)

All I can do is to trail meekly in the wake of the people who have been sent to Russia by Associations, Organizations, Societies and so on — and assimilate what I can from their comments and questions.

Then one day I remember that, before leaving England, I received a request written on a postcard.

Would I find out whether the lighter side of Russian life included the keeping of domestic pets. Cats and dogs and birds, said the postcard. They were never mentioned, it pointed out, in any of the books about Russia.

Did they exist, or not?

I think that, if I choose to make it mine, I can have this field of enquiry all to myself. Nobody else has so much as mentioned the subject.

Not that I intend to mention it, either. Neither Intourist nor my fellow travellers would think any the better of mine if I were suddenly to announce:

"As an observer of everyday life, I am interested in the Soviet reaction to the domestic cat. I wish to inspect a Home for Lost Dogs."

The best I can achieve is to look about me, and see what kind of appearance the domestic animals present.

The result of my investigation is discouraging.

The few dogs that I see are almost all of them farm dogs. At least, they live on farms. The best one can say about them is that they look—some of them—rather like dogs.

I see hardly any cats. None that bear any appearance of being household pets, poor creatures.

Birds I see—not many, I am thankful to say—in dreadful little cages scarcely bigger than themselves, hanging up outside the windows of some of the new dwelling-houses.

So I suppose I may take it that the lighter side of Russian life does *not* include the cherishing of pet animals.

Nor is it very surprising.

The housing problem is acute everywhere, and especially in Moscow. People who are obliged to live four or five in a single room, or at best in two, are scarcely likely to wish to add gratuitously to the existing congestion. I am not sure, either, if food is plentiful enough to admit of scraps being thrown to animals.

On the whole, my investigations on the position of the domestic pet in the Soviet State leave me unaccountably depressed. Perhaps it is because the pet animals at home have been the innocent occasions of so much fun, have taken part in so many family activities, have been so loved and loving, and sometimes so faithfully mourned, that one feels as if yet another of the minor graces of existence has been banished out of Russia with the new régime.

Then, at Odessa — the last, and nicest, of the places that I visit—the gloom lightens.

In the hotel there lives a kitten.

I VISIT THE SOVIETS

A grey, stubbly-haired, lively, very young kitten.

It is a thoroughly proletarian kitten—an infant Comrade. Its existence is supposed to be entirely confined to the dining-room, and the adjoining garden—which is really part of the dining-room— and it is there that it and I meet daily.

Sometimes I feed it, sometimes it sits on my lap, purring, sometimes it pretends to back away from me in a state of acute terror and retreats under the next-door table.

The waiters despise it. (I don't believe they would, if it was an aristocratic, long-haired kitten. Most of them are quite elderly waiters, and this used to be a place where the rich and the noble stayed, in the old days.)

When they find out that I like it, they pick the kitten up by its head and drop it contemptuously onto my knee.

The one great friend of the kitten — the one that, if it were Miss Blake, it would certainly call Me Friend—is a huge hall-porter, who sits outside the dining-room door and very slowly and unwillingly gets up whenever anybody passes in or out. Often and often I see the grey kitten racing up and down his enormous arm, or sitting on the palm

[271]

of his hand.

The hall-porter and I, on these occasions, silently exchange an indulgent smile, like grandparents watching a gambolling infant. When other visitors, particularly Russian ones, go past, he is apt to try and conceal the tiny creature, or to look as though he hadn't really noticed its presence.

One day, I witness his discomfiture.

It is 4 o'clock in the afternoon and the diningroom is therefore filled with visitors, all having the meal that in the U.S.S.R. is called dinner.

The orchestra, which never dreams of playing Russian music but devotes the whole of its tremendous energies to American jazz, is crashing its way through "Sous les Toits de Paris" in compliment to a party of French visitors who are occupying the largest table.

(What an extraordinarily popular tune this is, in Russia! I have heard it from every orchestra in every hotel. Perhaps it has only just arrived here?)

Then the gigantic hall-porter appears in the doorway, uniform and all, and stalks slowly up the long room, evidently to deliver a message at the far end of it.

I VISIT THE SOVIETS

The innocent grey kitten, perceiving its friend, prances out from nowhere to meet him—not straightforwardly, but with sidelong passes and pawings at the air, and every now and then rearing itself up and striking an attitude, like a ballet dancer of an undistinguished kind.

I have never seen anyone look more shocked than the hall-porter, at this untimely display. I can see him muttering the equivalent of "Not now, my dear fellow—not now" under his breath.

The kitten — less perceptive than I am — goes gaily on.

It is like seeing the chief official at a state function being jocosely hailed by a comic, rather vulgar friend.

I am sorry for the hall-porter.

He delivers his message, and walks down the room again, the grey kitten contorting itself at his heels.

"'T-ss—t-ss—t-ss——"

A waiter has flapped a napkin at it furiously, and the kitten shoots under the nearest table, which is mine.

I pick it up, and when I leave the dining-room take it with me, and hand it at the door to the hall-porter, who receives it with an air of infinite relief and gratitude.

With a benevolent smile I leave them to their explanation.

After that, the hall-porter gets up for me with more alacrity than he does for other people, and bestows upon me many an un-democratic bow as I go in and out.

This is practically the sum total of my special investigations into the question of pet animals in Russia. It is the best I can do, and not to be mentioned in the same breath as the probings into Conditions, Statistics and States of Affairs of my fellow tourists.

I perceive that, as a specialist, I am a failure.

It is not my line.

Or is it that I chose the wrong subject?

Would tractors, or prostitutes, have been better?

I shall never know.

THE ARISTOCRAT

IT OCCURS TO ME THAT MISS D. would look well on the steps of the guillotine. She would show to advantage there.

Here, she does not—trailing exhaustedly in the wake of a vigorous and aggressive young guide and a mixed lot—or Group—of tourists.

We are at Rostov-on-Don, and have been taken to inspect a factory of Agricultural Implements. It is very much my idea of Hell — hot and noisy and smelling most hideously, and with perilous-looking machinery grinding and clattering and whirling all over the place. Still, I can always amuse myself by counting the number of pictures of Stalin adorning the walls as we go through the different sheds, or by watching my fellow tourists.

On either side of the guide are two members of Agricultural Organizations—one Danish and one American—both of them looking at the machines as if they really liked seeing them, and knew quite a lot about their functions—as no doubt they do. The guide is, rightly, devoting most of her attention to them. That is to say, she shrieks explanations that are inaudible in the general clangings and crashings, and they bellow questions and comments of which not more than two words in ten can be heard by anybody.

The wife of the American comes next, tottering unhappily on very high-heeled shoes along floors that are slippery with oil and grease and water. Every now and then she tries to clutch at something, and has to give it up because nearly all the things with in reach are part of some machinery, and may either burn her, cut her to pieces, or whirl her bodily into some frightful collection of cogwheels.

She is paying no attention whatever to anything but her own distressing plight—and I don't blame her.

Two of her compatriots are behind her—a very young man with flaming red hair and a very illchosen scarlet pullover — and a quieter-looking contemporary. They are talking about Communism. I can't hear them, but they have talked of nothing else all day long, and have, I think, no other ideas in their heads at all.

Next to me is an Englishwoman, and she, also, is the product of an Organization, and seems to know all about farm implements.

I VISIT THE SOVIETS

Miss Blake and Miss Bolton are somewhere in the rear, probably continuing a discussion that they began in the auto-bus, about toothpaste.

And wandering about, all by herself, and never in the right aisle but always cut off from the rest of the group by some large engine, or impassable barrier of steel bars, or the angle of a machine, is Miss D.

It is then that I have my inspiration about how well she would look mounting the steps of the guillotine. She is neither young nor beautiful, but she is aristocratic.

Why in the world has she come to Russia?

Miss D. will, I think, never see forty again. She is tall, and very slight, and has limp, rather pretty brown hair, streaked with grey, and wavy, and falling about her head in a fashion neither smart nor modern. She has a beautiful nose: straight, and delicate. Her eyes are good too — in fact, if she only had some colour, or a little animation, she might pass as good-looking. She *is* good-looking, it suddenly occurs to me—but I doubt if anybody will ever notice it, especially if she persists in wearing a black frock with tiny little white daisies all over it, and a black hat shading her face.

I VISIT THE SOVIETS

She only arrived twenty-four hours ago, and has hardly spoken to anybody. At breakfast today I saw her reading *Jane Eyre* and thought well of her.

"The forges!" shrieks the guide.

Appalling-looking white-hot bars of iron are being snatched up in pincers off an iron slab, curved into unnatural shapes, and flung into a heap by smoke-blackened demons. The demons are female.

"The women, in the Soviet State, they do the same work as the men. They have the right," the guide yells triumphantly.

Roused to indignation, I yell back that it must be very bad for them.

"No. It is not bad for them."

Flat contradiction is amongst the favourite—but by no means the most endearing — accomplishments of the Intourist guides.

Unfortunately, it is rather catching.

"Yes, it is," I scream.

"No, no, it is not. It is very good for them. Besides, if a woman is——"

I know exactly what is coming next, and so does everybody else. It is as inevitable as Lenin's picture on the wall.

If a woman is expecting a baby, she does not

The smoke-blackened demons are females.

work for two months before it is born, nor for one month after, and she continues to receive full pay. It is a most excellent and humane scheme, only I don't want to hear about it *more* than seven times in any one week.

Besides, the heavy work at the forge must be a great tax on any woman's strength, even if she isn't expecting a baby.

I shake my head at the guide violently, to show her that I am still unconvinced—and then have to skip for my very life as a rattling trolley comes madly along the shed, apparently bent on our destruction. Miss Blake and Miss Bolton spring—the American lady in the high heels is swept into safety by her husband—and the guide first screams at Miss D. and then pushes her out of the trolley's reckless way.

"We must be careful," she cries.

We must, indeed—and so most of us are, except poor Miss D. who seems never to remember nor to realize where she is. We are continually having to retrieve her from wrong turnings, and divert her from the direct route of oncoming trolleys, and beg her, by signs, to remove herself from the immediate vicinity of flying sparks and the like.

Each time that I am able to hear her, she is saying "Thank you, thank you," to somebody who has just saved her from disaster.

There is a certain limp charm about her — and she has a nice smile—but how little sense!

One wonders what she can be doing alone in Russia. It is an unsuitable place for her.

Quite unlike most of one's fellow travellers, Miss D. has told nobody the story of her life. I know her name — which is rather a distinguished one—and that she has already been to Leningrad and Moscow and Kharkov, and is going on to the Crimea, and is all by herself.

The rest, so far, is silence.

I think that she has perhaps not been fortunate in her excursions this morning.

A picture gallery would have been much better, or a Museum, or even a Park of Rest and Culture. Not this incomprehensible, sulphur-smelling, clattering chaos.

We are shown the First Aid Station. Workers come here when they sustain injuries in the machine shops. (If Miss D. and I were engaged here, which Heaven forbid, we should never be out of the place.) They also inhale something-or-other, and gargle, when the sulphur becomes too much for them. The infirmarian in charge tells the guide, who tells me, that we may inhale and gargle, if we like. She seems surprised and disappointed when none of us accepts the offer.

Then we all go to the office. Miss D. gets lost on the way, and is angrily searched for by the guide, and retrieved from the workers' dining-room, which smells of sulphur and is enlivened by strains of jazz from a colossal loud-speaker.

In the office all the mechanically or agriculturally minded tourists ask questions and write the answers down in note-books.

The American lady looks disconsolately at her shoes, which besides having nearly cost her her life in the machine-sheds, have obviously been ruined by oil and grease, and the two American youths smoke fiercely, to make up for having been unable to do so during the inspection.

Miss Blake and Miss Bolton are listening attentively to everything the guide says.

They always do.

How conscientious they are!

They go everywhere, they listen to everything, they take notes on every possible subject, from the

[281]

tomb of Stalin's wife to the price of toilet-paper in Moscow.

Sometimes I wonder what they are going to do with all their information.

Perhaps, when they get home, they will read Papers about the Soviet State to Literary Societies. Or perhaps they will just look through their notes, in the long winter evenings, and either wish themselves back in Russia, or feel thankful to be safely out of it.

Or they may just talk it all over together.

"Do you remember, Bolton, exactly how many tractors left Rostov in the first six months of 1935?"

"It's in my note-book, Blake. I knew I should want those figures, sooner or later."

Miss D., unlike Miss Blake and Miss Bolton, is not conscientious. I have my doubts whether she is even listening.

What *has* she come for, I wonder?

Perhaps as a kind of endurance test, to see how much fatigue, discomfort and boredom her obviously frail physique can endure without collapsing? If she miscalculates, and *does* collapse, she will find herself in a Russian sanatorium, to which the chief drawback will be that privacy of any kind will be quite unobtainable, owing to lack of accommodation.

(I am led away into a fantasy about Miss D. lying in a state of collapse in hospital, with myself as a ministering angel coming to visit her and lending her *Bleak House* and *David Copperfield* and offering her my reserve piece of soap. I also undertake to telegraph to her relations in England, and allowing five words for the address—which is quite unknown to me—try to work out a telegram that shall be at once informative, reassuring, imperative and yet inexpensive.

It can't be done.

I must give up "no danger" and leave them to infer that she is in good hands (mine)—and that I am prepared to stay at her beside until they can arrive. If they have any decent feeling at all, they will come by air.)

"You wish to ask a question, yes?" says the guide abruptly—I think noticing my abstraction, and resenting it.

"I don't think so, thank you."

"I will answer anything you want to know."

"It's all beautifully clear," I reply. An answer

which, so far as I am concerned, is a perfectly flat lie. It isn't clear, and it never *could* be clear.

"Do ask something," says the American expert, very kindly and courteously. "I'm afraid I've been monopolizing the services of our guide."

I see that I shall have to evolve something. What in the name of fortune can I ask that will sound reasonably intelligent?

I feel like the young gentleman at Mr. Podsnap's dinner-party, madly saying "Esker——" to the Foreign Gentleman and then finding himself unable to proceed.

At last I enquire *exactly* what the proportion of women workers is—implying that only the most absolute accuracy on this point will satisfy me— and the guide translates the question and the answer, and honour is appeased. To do the thing perfectly, I ought to write down the figures in a note-book—but I don't.

Miss D. has asked nothing. Nobody seems to expect it of her. The guide looks at her, from time to time, in a dissatisfied way and once asks me— aside—if I know why she has come to Russia.

I do not: and if I did should see no reason for sharing my knowledge with Intourist's guides.

I VISIT THE SOVIETS

All the guides ask questions, about all the tourists, of all the other tourists. I think it is part of their job.

Presently we are all in the autobus again, going through the streets of Rostov. What a clean, cheerful town it is, by comparison with Moscow! There are flowering trees all along the boulevards, and plenty of shops, making a great show with extremely little, and even kiosks at some of the street corners, with flowers for sale. The Don lies below the town, in the midst of blue and green and grey marshes.

"The new theatre."

The new theatre is a fine building, designed on modern lines, and very well situated at the entrance of the town, overlooking the river. Even if it were none of these things, all of us except the most honest or the strongest-minded would emit polite exclamations of approval. We have got into the habit of it. The guide expects it of us. If we ever do, any of us, utter a breath of criticism she either ignores it, or flatly contradicts it. I therefore only say that the theatre reminds me of the new de la Warr Pavilion at Bexhill-on-Sea—which it does.

"Yes? You have one as large in England?" the

guide enquires in a most incredulous tone.

"Quite as large. Larger."

"Ah, that is very good," she replies, in a patronizing manner.

Miss Bolton says to me:

"Do you know Bexhill-on-Sea?"

I say Yes, and refrain from adding that if I didn't I naturally shouldn't have made the comparison.

"The cousin of a friend of mine has a very nice house near Bexhill," says Miss Bolton.

I feel that she thinks the better of me for this rather unsubstantial link between us.

"I've never been there myself, but I've often heard this friend talk about her cousin's place. She stays there sometimes."

The air at Bexhill, I suggest, is very good.

Oh, very.

Very, says Miss Blake, adding the weight of her testimonial.

"You have a good air, at the sea, in England?" asks the guide, as incredulously as ever.

Excellent air. Splendid. Magnificent.

We are all very emphatic on the point, and are handsomely supported by the American couple who have probably never been to Bexhill-on-Sea in their lives, but evidently realize that the guide's assumption that no good air can exist outside the Soviet Union requires squashing.

Needless to say, she remains unimpressed. "In Odessa," she informs us, "the climate is very good. It gives health. There are many, many houses there, once belonging to rich people, that are now all made into sanatoria. The workers are sent there by the Government for one month, two months, when they are found by the doctors to require a rest."

"And what has happened to the rich people—the ones to whom the houses belonged?"

The guide looks shocked at my enquiry, as though it was of a slightly indecent character.

She replies with reserve that some of them have left Russia, and that others have conformed to the new Government. They have become workers. I ponder this in silence, thinking of some of the rich people I know in England and wondering what kind of workers they would turn into, under a Soviet régime.

"This house, belonging to this cousin of a friend of mine, is on the Hastings side of the town," remarks Miss Bolton.

And I say "Ah, is it!" is though that made all the difference to my estimate of the house, the cousin and Bexhill-on-Sea generally.

Russia, undoubtedly, conduces very little towards constructive and intelligent intercourse amongst fellow-travellers.

It might, I think, be interesting to hear Miss D. talk, but this is exactly what she never does. She only says "Thank you" when people extricate her from the difficulties into which she is continually falling, and occasionally "Good-night" or "Good-morning."

What would happen to Miss D. in a Soviet State? She is pathetically ineffectual. I doubt whether she could become a worker in the Soviet sense of the word, under any consideration whatsoever. Yet at a guess I should say she lived in the country, in a house and on land owned by her forbears for generations, and now probably heavily mortgaged, and that she devotes herself unsparingly and quite effectively to a great number of undertakings for the betterment of her village friends and neighbours.

I am again obliged to think, this time most unwillingly, of the steps of the guillotine. I know that

Miss D. would mount them calmly and with dignity and that, though she stumbled in the machine-sheds, she wouldn't stumble there.

But I also know that I don't want to see her there, either literally or metaphorically.

And just then we arrive at the Hotel, and as we go in at the door the red-headed American boy stands back to let me pass, and then spoils the effect by remarking that it's funny how we still retain our bourgeois standards of politeness.

I tell him in return, rather grimly, that he will no doubt enjoy the tramcars in Moscow where nothing whatever in the nature of bourgeois standards prevails, and the older and feebler members of the proletariat get heartily shoved and kicked out of the way by the younger and stronger. But he is young and strong himself, so naturally the methods of the Moscow Comrades will suit him better than they did me.

After all, I do hear Miss D. talk.

She is talking in French, quite beautifully and without any trace of English at all.

Just as I thought.

She is accomplished , without being efficient.

[289]

Her French conversation is on behalf of an angry old gentleman, English, who wishes to have his room changed. The English-speaking guides are out, and he can speak no word of any language but his own. Miss D. is translating for him, at the Bureau. That is to say, she is putting his torrents of abuse into short phrases, expressive of a polite desire for some slight improvement as regards noise, cockroaches and a defective hot-water tap in his bedroom.

Naturally, she accomplishes nothing. Her manner—which would do so well in diplomatic circles—is of no avail at all in dealing with hotel employees, who are exactly the same all the world over.

They despise Miss D. at sight. They know that it will always be possible to "put upon" her, that she is morally incapable of disputing a flagrant over-charge, and that she will put up with quite unnecessary discomforts from sheer want of knowing how to remedy them. Never will Miss D. insist upon "having her money's worth"—as of course she ought to do. She doesn't know what her money's worth *is*.

Not so very many generations back, I imagine, the ancestors of Miss D. went gaily through life, ordering what they wanted and paying for it when or if convenient—always generous, and seldom just—and never for one moment disputing that the ruling places of the earth should be theirs by Divine right.

Miss D. is the strange product of this heredity, and of present-day environment.

She is neither one thing nor the other.

One sees it with singular clarity against the Russian background.

"You are interested in Hospitals, yes?"

"Oh yes."

It would be a poor look-out for me if I wasn't, as there have been Hospitals, of one kind or another, on the programme of every Intourist Bureau in every town that I have yet visited.

As a matter of fact, I am interested.

On this occasion apparently nobody else is, except Miss D., and we have a guide all to ourselves. It is the blonde, aggressive one—not the nice little Austrian one, whom we all like. The Hospital turns out to be a Maternity Hospital and Gynecological Clinic. The building is good, and situated in a garden. On arrival we and the guide are thrust into cleanish white overalls—in which we look like some degraded species of overgrown choir-boy—as a hygienic precaution. It is not really a very whole-hearted one, as quite a large area of each one of us still remains uncovered, and quite possibly swarming with germs. But a similar ritual always prevails, and always provokes the naïve pride and admiration of the guides. A woman doctor—how she must resent the interruption to her morning's work!—comes to show us round.

Compared with an English or an American Hospital the wards are dingy, cheerless, and, above all, appallingly over-crowded. But the comparison is an unfair one and I *must* remember not to make it.

Compared with pre-Revolution accommodation, I have no doubt that what we are seeing now represents a vast improvement.

A chorus of thin, shrill squawkings introduces us to the ward in which dozens—literally dozens —of brand-new human beings are lying, protesting against their arrival into the world. Most of them are muffled to the eyebrows in shawls and blankets. Impossible not to wonder if anyone can really ever tell any of them apart.

Have they all got identity disks?

No, they are all entered in a book.

I don't think—knowing, as I do, the dilatori-ness of Russian methods—that this reply is wholly satisfactory.

Then we see a convalescent ward. Again, the beds are terribly close together, and there are a very great number of them. We learn that each woman is discharged from Hospital a week after giving birth to her child, unless exceptional com-plications have arisen. The beds are urgently required, and there are not enough of them.

Is there any after-care?

Yes, there is a clinic to which the mother can go, and to which they can take the babies for advice, and there are trained Social Workers who visit them in their own homes.

"There are two of our Social Workers, over there," says the guide. "They are resting."

The Social Workers wear nurse's uniform.

They have a curiously unofficial, inefficient appearance. Their white head-dresses are innocent of starch, and their overalls are not clean. Neither, unfortunately, are their hands—and one of them has seen fit to smear her nails with a frightful dark-red varnish. They would inspire me with so little confidence, were I the object of their visitations, that I should without hesitation show them the door.

How, I wonder, is Miss D. taking all this?

She is looking worried, and gazing distressfully at a row of waiting women, most of them with children beside them, who are sitting crowded together on an inadequate little bench.

The guide takes us down another passage. I miss the smell of disinfectant associated with Hospitals at home. I have never liked it before, but now I think that I should be quite glad to meet it again.

The doctor who is leading the way pushes open a door, and signs to us to go in.

At first, I think I am in another ward. There are two nurses standing about, doing nothing, and there are eight or nine patients on the beds . . . only they aren't beds. . . .

Suddenly I understand.

They have taken us, sight-seeing, into the labour ward.

The guide seems unable to understand why

I VISIT THE SOVIETS

Miss D. and I have backed out of the ward so precipitately.

"But do you always take tourists in there?"

"Why not? We have nothing to hide."

"Don't the women *mind?*"

"I do not know. They do not say."

"In England, only one patient at a time goes into the labour ward. Never several of them all together."

"They hadn't even got screens," says Miss D. in a low voice. Her face is very green—and I rather think that mine is too.

"What for, screens?" says the guide in an interested way.

It would be waste of words to talk to her about privacy. The word, in Russia, has no meaning at all—and the thing itself does not, so far as I have seen, exist.

Presently Miss D. and I find ourselves out again in the fresh air—of which we are both slightly in need.

We exchange very few comments on the morning's sight-seeing.

Only Miss D. asks me, in awed tones, whether I

think we should have been taken into the labour ward just the same if we had been, as we so often are, part of a large mixed group of tourists.

I am bound to say that I feel sure we should.

Miss D., after a long silence, observes that her Women's Institute at home has expressed great interest in her visit to Russia, and that she hopes to give them a little talk about it on her return, but some of her experiences will have to be left out.

I tell her in return that precisely the same consideration has already occurred to me on my own account

"Are you interested in Women's Institutes?"

"Very."

We settle down into a thoroughly agreeable conversation about the Women's Institute movement, and on the whole I enjoy the next half-hour better than I have enjoyed most things in Russia.

All I learn about Miss D.—besides her connection with Women's Institutes—is that she lives in the country (just as I thought) in Warwickshire, and came to Russia because she wished to see for herself what Communism was really like.

Her conclusion appears to be much the same as my own: that Russian Communism, taking it bye and large, is probably an improvement on Russian Imperialism, and that we r ust, like Mr. Twemlow, hold on to that. Otherwise, we shall be tempted to condemn it wholesale as a reversion to barbarism.

I only have two more conversations with Miss D.

One is when I meet her again, unexpectedly, in Odessa, whither she has come from the Crimea and from whence she intends to sail for Bucharest. She is distressed and helpless under the persistent conversation of a Ukrainian gentleman who has lived twenty years in America and prides himself on speaking English exactly like an American—which he doesn't and never will. At best, he might hope to be mistaken for a Polish taxi-driver from New York.

A singular ambition.

He and Miss D. travelled together in the same railway carriage, and I gather that this has seemed to the Ukrainian to constitute a reason for sitting at the table next to hers at every meal and bombarding her with information about Odessa as he knew it twenty years ago.

"This hotel was kind of a luxury hotel, where the million-dollar Grafs and all like that brought their fancy dames. Did the champagne flow—oh boy! I guess some of the waiters wish them days was back again all right all right. You bet your life they do. Some of them was here then, holding open the doors, and bowing like they was some kind of Eastern slave, and helping the Dukes and Grafs and all like that on with their coats, and getting five-dollar bills handed out to them like it was so much waste-paper. I guess they think those were the days."

"Nobody tips them now?"

"No, siree, nobody certainly don't. The Soviet has put an end to all that. They work for a fixed wage, like anybody else, and nobody don't give them nothing. I guess that's why they look kind of sour. They're just a bunch of old-timers, mostly, and they can't get used to the new ways. That's the way I figure it out, leastways. I guess it's kind of natural."

I guess it is, too, and I think Miss D. does.

The waiters, now one comes to look at them, are most of them old. They are also very, very slow— but all Russian waiters are that.

The immense length of time that elapses in the dining-room between sitting down at a table and giving an order—and then between each course—gives the Ukrainian gentleman almost unlimited opportunity for talk, and he always takes full advantage of it.

Miss D. wilts, and looks wretched, but is unable to get rid of him. To do that would, I think, require a brutal candour of which she is hopelessly incapable.

So, unfortunately, am I.

We are privileged to assist, as unwilling spectators, at a fearful scene which he makes one morning, with the oldest of all the old waiters, because the toast ordered with his breakfast tea is hard.

(It is—hard as a brick. So was mine, so, I feel sure, was everybody's. It always is.)

The Ukrainian is very angry—perhaps justly. He is also very noisy and abusive in Russian. He thumps the table and roars.

The aged waiter mutters a little in reply, and looks unspeakably sullen.

The toast is removed. The Ukrainian thumps the table and roars again, this time in English.

Hours later the waiter reappears with the same toast, harder and colder than ever.

Miss D. and I, simultaneously, retreat before the storm.

What a mercy it is that the Ukrainian gentleman is leaving this very night! and how heartily I hope that I need never again set eyes on him. Miss D. has ascertained that he is not going to Bucharest, but to Istanbul. If there were any possibility of their meeting once more, I think she would alter her itinerary on the spot.

Next morning I hold my final conversation with her.

She has got her breakfast: I am still waiting for mine.

"Good Heavens! Your toast is quite hot! Then that odious man did have some effect, after all?"

"I'm afraid," says Miss D. gently and apologetically, "that my toast always has been hot. At least, it has for several days."

"Did you——?"

"Yes," says Miss D. "I tipped the waiter. It was only a very little tip. They tell you that tipping is forbidden, and that no one accepts anything like that, in the Soviet,—but the waiter accepted it at once. He has looked after me very well indeed since then."

And he bows to the earth whenever he sees her. I have noticed it myself.

I say, without any great originality, that it looks as though human nature hadn't altered very much, even in the Soviet.

Miss D. agrees with me politely.

She adds, with her deprecating smile:

"The funny thing is that I didn't do it because of the toast or anything. I just did it because, after what that dreadful Ukrainian told us about the poor waiters remembering the old days, I felt so sorry for them.

INCIDENT AT ODESSA

IF THERE IS ONE THING THAT IS MORE frequently impressed upon the tourist than any other in the U.S.S.R., it is that in Russia there are no prostitutes.

Naturally, one can only congratulate one's informants on so gratifying a state of affairs. It is, perhaps, a pity that the guides should announce it quite so aggressively—as who should say: How different from the deplorable state of affairs in Capitalist countries—but after all, one is used to that. The guides, though nearly always obliging and conscientious, are apt to display an aggressive manner.

Perhaps it is part of their training, which must be a very odd and a very intensive one.

Most of them speak at least two foreign languages fluently, and with an astonishing command of the technical expressions necessary for explanations in factories, hospitals, museums and the like. I could wish that they hadn't all been taught to reply, when thanked, with "Don't mention it," and that they didn't repeat one's name with every other sentence, but these, after all, are

[302]

conversational drawbacks that are also sometimes to be met with in England.

It is significant that almost all the guides are very young. That is to say, they have been born and bred under the new régime, and its merits have been held up for their admiration ever since they can remember anything at all. I have only met one who has ever been outside Russia. All the others have learnt their language in Moscow, at schools or universities. They have, with regard to standards of living and of culture, nothing with which to compare the Soviet Union.

Their enthusiasm is, I think, genuine—as well it may be, since it has been strenuously ground into them from infancy—but its value is discounted by their lack of any sense of proportion.

No country—least of all one that has so recently emerged from civil war as has Russia—can be as advanced, as prosperous, as perfect, as the guides tell us that the U.S.S.R. now is.

No countries, I trust, can be as barbarous, as benighted and as contemptible as the guides assert —at least by implication—all Capitalist countries to be.

They do not say or imply this because they wish

to be unpleasant. They say it because they have been told to say it, and they obviously believe it to be true.

They have a superb set of formulas, which have varied not at all in any of the towns that I, or any other tourist that I meet, have visited.

"In the Soviet Union there are no prostitutes."

"There is no unemployment."

"There is enough food for everybody."

"Everybody is happy. Nobody wishes to go away. They are free, if they wish, to go—but they do not wish."

"Everybody is equal."

Of these statements, I believe the second one without reservation.

I do *not* believe an ultra-enthusiastic guide who is taking me over a children's school in Kharkov.

"What do you do with your problem children?"

"Problem children?"

"Difficult children. Those who don't mix well with the others, or give trouble."

"Ah. Nervous ones."

"Perhaps. Yes."

"In the Soviet State we have no nervous children," serenely asserts the guide. "They have no what you call com*plexes*."

"No complexes? Not any at all, ever?"

"Never."

Naturally, that simplifies the problem of dealing with them.

Very few of the tourists have enough courage to argue with the guides, even when they set forth the most preposterous claims.

"Since the Revolution, we have scarcely any illness in Russia."

"Since the Revolution, creative art in Russia is becoming realistic altogether. It is much better."

Nobody says:

"But is it?" or "How do you know?"

I often *think* it—but I don't say it.

The guides have it all their own way.

They have formulas for dealing with inconvenient requests and enquiries also.

"Today it is shut. We cannot see."

"Could we go there tomorrow?"

"I do not know."

"Perhaps it would be possible to telephone and find out?"

"Perhaps."

"I am particularly anxious to go there, and I

[305]

leave the day after tomorrow."

"It will perhaps be possible to arrange."

I can't remember which of the French kings it was who always, when asked to do what he had rather not do, replied: *Le roi s'avisera.* I often think of him.

(I don't suppose the guides would like to be compared to a French king at all.)

There is another dialogue that I hear, with very slight variations, in many places.

"You would like to visit one of the apartments for the workers, yes?"

"Very much. Would they mind, if we went inside?"

"No, no, they are delighted."

"*This* one, then?"

"No, *that* one it will be better."

The guide invariably has her eye on the particular establishment that is to be visited, and the suggestions of the visitor are ignored.

No fair-minded person can reasonably find fault. It is a concession to be allowed inside anybody's dwelling at all, and so one feels it. But it is quite absurd to pretend, as the guides invariably do, that every dwelling is freely open to inspection,

[306]

and that mere blind chance has led us into one rather than another.

Everything is *not* open to inspection in Russia, and why indeed should it be? Only, one would like to urge, let us have no meandering about it. As it is, the verbal meanderings of the guides are both annoying and unconvincing, besides giving the inevitable impression that, as my Savoyard fellow traveller so frequently and so passionately exclaimed: *On nous cache quelque chose.*

Once, and only once, I am privileged to behold two of the Intourist guides behaving like natural young proletarians instead of like amateur young Machiavellis.

We are on the beach, at Odessa.

It is a picturesque beach, on the Black Sea, with rocks on one side of the little bay, and gardens and a park above it. The sun is blazing down on the blue water, and on the incredible number of people lying and sitting and standing and splashing about.

Why are nearly all the male Comrades so thin and all the female ones so stout? Of course, their system of going in to bathe clad only in a brassière and a pair of drawers fails to show them to the greatest advantage—one must remember that.

I VISIT THE SOVIETS

On some beaches, all the Comrades bathe together in the nude—but not on this one. I can,
from an aesthetic point of view, only be glad of it.

There are no bathing-cabins. We undress as
gracefully as we can and no one appears to find
decency very difficult except one American Jewess,
who screams a good deal and requests the guides
to stand in front of her, and her husband to turn
his back—which compels him to confront me, in
an equal state of déshabillé.

However, I remove myself into the water as
speedily as possible and try to find some square
inch of it that is not wholly encumbered by the legs
and arms of the Comrades who seem all to be—
like myself—poor and ineffectual swimmers.

Close beside me a Venus of terrifying proper-
tions, rises from the foam and admires, in broken
English, my blue rubber bathing-cap.

I see why. Her own large head of brass-coloured
ridges is ill-adapted to salt water, and in Russia I
know that rubber goods are not to be found. (I
have learnt this from the universal and loud-spoken
lamentations of the Comrades on the impossibility
of obtaining contraceptives.)

I tell her that I got the bathing-cap in London,

[308]

Why are nearly all the male Comrades so thin and all the female ones so stout?

and hope I don't sound aggressively triumphant. Russia and the guides between them drive one to boastful ways, too often.

Venus has never been to London. Her husband is an Englishman.

(I think I see why she has never been to London.)

She asks if I speak Russian.

Very little. But she, of course, speaks English?

No, she has never really learnt it.

Triumphing over this disability she continues to talk to me at intervals, in a strange mixture of tongues. Her conversational *cheval de bataille* in English is "Mai Gahd!" which she screams aloud whenever a drop of water splashes the upper part of her person.

I nod, and swim away, and think of Alice and the Mouse in the pool of tears.

When, eventually, I leave the water, Venus leaves it also and comments on my bathing-suit. I can think of nothing to say about hers in return, except that it is very inadequate, so content myself with nodding and smiling.

"Mai Gahd!" says Venus reflectively, and begins to remove her brassière—which is as dry as a

[309]

bone.

I return to my clothes, over which the guides are sitting—having informed me that it will not be wise to leave them unguarded for one moment. (I am bound to say that I afterwards many times disproved this altogether, when I went by myself to the same beach to bathe.)

The guides are agitated.

What is the matter?

Nothing, they say in tones of the most sinister significance.

Has the American Jewess been drowned, or is her husband objecting to the extreme publicity of their dressing and undressing?

No. The American Jewess, in a most elaborate green swimming-suit, all laced up with white, is sitting on the sand looking with great disfavour at the sea, and the husband, in bathing-trunks and a pair of dark-glasses, is lying flat on his back beside her.

The guides mutter together like conspirators and cast furious glances over their shoulders.

Presently the elder one, whom the other one calls Katya, gets up and walks over to the brass-haired Venus. I can't hear what she says—she is speaking quietly. But Venus, in reply, shrieks "Mai Gahd!" in tones that ring through the bay.

In less than two seconds they are in the midst of a most terrific quarrel, and the younger guide has rushed up to support Katya.

I do not rush, but I creep, as unobtrusively as possible, within hearing distance. I want to know what it is all about, and I am interested in seeing the guides quite off their guard and say to myself dramatically:

Nature in the raw.

It wouldn't be very difficult to understand what the antagnonists are saying—or screaming—even if I knew much less Russian than I do.

Katya has lodged an objection because the brass-haired Venus permitted herself to enter into conversation with me, a tourist.

Venus is furious—perhaps not unnaturally—at being told, by a complete stranger, that she may not speak to another complete stranger.

She says that she will speak to whom she likes and, alternatively, that she spoke not one word. She adds something that I do not understand but that is obviously highly vituperative.

Katya replies—I am certain of it—the Russian

equivalent of: "Call yourself a lady!"

By this time quite a circle of Comrades has gathered round. Two young men are being appealed to by the guides. Why? They have had nothing to do with any of it. The supporters of Venus are an elderly woman with a sardonic laugh —which she emits with great effect at short, regular intervals—two naked children, and a bony youth in a pair of blue shorts and spectacles.

A curious, rather somnambulistic effect is imparted to the whole scene by the fact that Venus, throughout, continues to take off the things she wore in the sea and to put on others—fastening and unfastening, and stepping in and out, while she screams at the guides and they scream at her.

No—one is unjust. Only Katya screams.

The little guide, the younger and more intelligent of the two, does not scream. She gathers herself together, and when there is a moment's lull she utters. She is much too rapid and fluent for me to follow her—but oh, how well I know that tone! How well I know that note of withering sarcasm, that mock-politeness, that brief and utterly mirthless Ha-ha-ha! with which the speech is brought to its vibrant close. It is the selfsame speech that, in England, ends with a reference to the marriage lines of the antagonist.

The little guide, having shot her bolt, turns her back, sits down on the sand, and begins to cry.

The two young men stand over her and look solemn but say nothing. How wise they are!

Venus and all her supporters retire to a distance and exchange observations, in loud, clarion tones, all about the guides—but not directly addressed to them.

Katya says:

"She is an insulting woman."

Nothing could be more evident. We are all, more or less, being insulting women, and I should be glad if we might now bring the whole thing to a close.

The American Jews, who haven't understood a word—unless they identified "Mai Gahd!"—try to get an explanation from Katya, and don't succeed, and I approach the little tearful guide and suggest that she should stop crying.

"Oh, I cry not. I laugh," she replies haughtily, but untruthfully, and with streaming eyes.

"Why should I cry, for such a woman? She is a prostitute. Nothing but a prostitute."

[313]

What an opportunity for replying: "But I thought that in Russia there were no prostitutes!"

But of course I don't.

I merely philosophize intelligently to myself on the discovery that this age-old term of abuse has not been ousted, even by the Soviet Government, from human nature's repertory.

"No better than she should be."

In cold blood, the guides, I feel sure, would die before admitting the existence of prostitutes, individually or collectively, anywhere in the New Russia. But when they cease to be guides, and revert to their real type, how naturally it comes out!

Everybody else leaves the beach in a battered condition, and I pretend to be battered too—but actually, am rather interested and triumphant. Especially when the guides, after talking a great deal about witnesses, and libel, and Courts of Law, become thoughtful and exhausted and finally declare that "it will perhaps be better to say nothing and forget."

They mean, say nothing to the Intourist Bureau at the hotel, and this I readily undertake.

As for forgetting—Never!

This, however, I do not tell them. Not even on

the next occasion when I hear them asserting that:
In Russia there are no prostitutes.

TO SPEAK MY MIND

(1)

THE TIME HAS COME FOR ME TO speak my mind as to what I feel about the Soviet Republic.

But to whom?

My fellow travellers all have opinions of their own which they regard, rightly or wrongly, as being of more value than mine. Most of them are pessimistic, and declare that they don't ever want to come back again, and that the Crimea was lovely but the plugs in the hotels wouldn't pull, and Moscow was interesting but very depressing.

Some, on the other hand—like Mrs. Pansy Baker—are wholly enthusiastic. (There is no *juste milieu* where the Soviet is concerned.) How splendid it all is, they cry, and how fine to see everybody busy, happy and cared-for. As for the institutions—the crèches, the schools, the public parks and the prisons—all, without any qualification whatsoever, are perfect. Russia has nothing left to learn.

It would be idle to argue with them. For the

matter of that, it is almost always idle to argue with anybody.

In Russia, it is not only idle but practically impossible.

One had thought of Russia, in one's out-of-date bourgeois way, as a country of tremendous discussions—of long evenings spent in splendid talk round the samovar—of abstract questions thrashed out between earnest thinkers. All that must have gone out with the Grand Dukes, the beautiful women, the borzois, the sables and the diamonds.

The Comrades do not discuss: they assert. They contradict.

They admit of no criticism whatever.

Nothing could be more difficult nor, probably, more unprofitable than to speak one's mind in Russia concerning one's impressions of Russia.

But all the same, I shall try. After all, it's my turn. For weeks and weeks I have followed meekly in the wake of pert and rather aggressive young women, who have told me how vastly superior everything in the U.S.S.R. is to everything in my own Capitalistic country (where they have never set foot).

And although several of the guides have been

neither pert nor aggressive, but very obliging and friendly, even they have smiled rather pityingly at any comment other than one of unqualified approval.

In fact the U.S.S.R., like the Pope, is infallible, and whereas the Pope's claim has at least the dignity of some two thousand years of experience behind it, that of the U.S.S.R. has not.

I shall speak my mind before I leave the country. I am resolved upon it. And I shall have to do it fairly soon, too. Odessa is my last stopping-place. A Russian boat is to take me to Constantinople in a week's time. The new Mrs. Trollope is, figuratively speaking, turning her back on the bazaar and the pincushions.

There is a very intelligent Russian in the hotel: he is a doctor, and has lived for several years in the United States.

I shall speak my mind to the Russian doctor.

We often sit at the same table for breakfast. Surely he would welcome an impartial discussion on the state of his country, from an intelligent visitor?

"I shall be leaving next week. I am going to Turkey, and then back to England. Everything

I have seen in Russia has been most interesting."

This is not perhaps literally true—but then, so very few statements ever are. After the first fifty, for instance, none of the pictures of Lenin and Stalin were in the least interesting. But it will do, I think, to start the impartial discussion.

"You find Soviet Russia interesting? Yes, that is what everybody says."

Well, it wasn't a very original opening. I see that now, and wish that I had thought of something new and brilliant instead.

"But," says the Russian doctor, "it is quite impossible for you to form any correct opinion of the country unless you knew it before the Revolution."

Then I've been wasting the whole of my time?

"No one can judge of the New Russia who did not know intimately, over a period of many years, and from the inside, the Old Russia."

The only reply I can think of to this is Good God! and I do not make it aloud. But really, if I left home and children and country, and spent months of discomfort in places I haven't liked, and generally tried to emulate Mrs. Trollope, only to learn at the end of it all that none of my collected impressions are of any value whatever, it does seem rather discouraging. The Russian doctor is either unaware of, or indifferent to, the blow that he has dealt.

"Many people make that mistake," he remarks sombrely. "They think that because they have visited a few museums, schools, hospitals, with an interpreter, they know something about this country. They do not. They know *nothing*."

In that case I ought to get a refund from Intourist. They sent me out here on entirely false pretences.

"Another thing," continues the doctor, evidently warming to his work, "not only is it impossible to know anything about Soviet Russia without a profound knowledge of Russia under the Tsars, it is also *absolutely* impossible to judge of it in any way correctly at the present date. For that, you would have to come again, say in twenty years' time."

How unreasonable he is. If I come to Russia again in twenty years' time—which God forbid— it will be in a bath-chair.

"So it would really take a whole lifetime," I dejectedly suggest, "to understand exactly what is happening in the Soviet?"

"More than a lifetime. Two or three generations."

I give up, altogether, the idea of speaking my mind about the U.S.S.R. to the Russian doctor.

I must find somebody else.

I am inspired to choose one of the Odessa Intourist guides. She has a more pliable outlook than most of them, and is married to an Austrian husband. She has been abroad, to France and Austria and America.

"Did you like America?"

"Yeah, America was fine."

"Perhaps some day you will go back there. Would you like to go back?"

"Perhaps. But it is not a free country."

"Not a free country?"

"The workers there are slaves. The women are slaves," says the guide firmly.

"I really don't think they are. American women always seem to me to have a great deal of liberty."

"No. They have no liberty. They cannot do the work that the men do."

"But I don't think they want to."

"In the Socialist state, a woman is the equal of a man in every way. She can become a mechanic,

[321]

an engineer, a bricklayer, a mason. If she is expecting a child, she does no work for two months
before and one month after it is born, and she gets
her money just the same while she is nursing the
child—"

I know all this. I have heard it, and more than
once, from every guide in every town that I have
visited. The treatment of the expectant mother is
the *cheval de bataille* of the whole Soviet system—
and a very respectable *cheval*, too—but it cannot,
surely, be the answer to every question—the
triumphant last word in every discussion?

"I think the care that the Government takes of
mothers and children in Russia is most excellent
—but on the other hand, there is not very much
individual freedom for women in the upbringing
of their children. It is all, really, in the hands of
the State."

"The children are very happy. You have seen the
crèches, the little beds for them to sleep on, in the
day-time, yes? Each child has its own toothbrush."

"I know. But the mothers don't see very much
of them, do they, if they only have them home at
night?"

"In the day-time they are at work. They have

the right to work."

"Supposing they didn't want to work, and would rather look after their children at home?"

"Some of the women become Stakhanovite workers. Then they have privileges given to them —an extra room, or a wireless, or perhaps a car. We have many like that."

Yes, I know that too. In every factory there is a board, bearing photographs of the Stakhanovite workers—who are usually distinguished for their capability rather than for their looks.

I cannot help feeling that the guide is not keeping to the point of the discussion—or even trying to do so.

"The experiment that is being tried over here is most interesting, but it seems to me to allow very little scope for individuality. Isn't that one of the drawbacks to the Communist system?"

"There are no drawbacks to the Communist system."

One looks at her in mingled admiration and despair. Admiration because she has been drilled into such blind and stubborn loyalty to her employers, and despair because it is so obviously impossible to conduct any discussion on such a basis.

I make one more effort.

"But surely there must be a few drawbacks to every system to begin with, until it has been perfected. For instance, the complete lack of privacy must be trying, such a number of people all living in one, or two, rooms. Even in the hospitals. I suppose there's no such thing as a private ward."

"Here in Odessa, on the way to the sea, the houses that used to belong to rich people have all been converted into sanatoria for the workers. Those who need it are sent out here for a month, two months, as they require, by their trades-unions."

"I know. I've seen them."

"There are beautiful gardens to those houses. They can sit there. And they can go and bathe in the sea."

"That's splendid. Do the workers who need a holiday choose where they go, or is it settled for them?"

"They are told by the Government where to go for their holidays."

"That's what I meant. There isn't a great deal of freedom. Don't some of them feel they'd rather decide those things for themselves?"

"Sometimes the doctor orders special treatment. We have near here very celebrated mud-baths that cure all kinds of rheumatism."

It is like a conversation from an old-fashioned travel-book:

" 'Where is the band-box containing hats of which I asked you to take care, you good-for-nothing fellow?' "

" 'Sir, if you and your lady will rest awhile at the Inn, there is a fine view of Mont Blanc to be obtained from the parlour window.' "

Nothing is to be gained by going on talking with the guide.

I shall have to speak my mind elsewhere.

But how difficult it is. Russians do not want one to speak one's mind. It is true that they like to talk, but they do not in the least like to listen. Least of all, do they like to listen to criticism of any kind.

Well, perhaps they have their reasons for that. I only once go so far as to ask the lady who shows us round a Palace of the Pioneers in Rostov whether she would not like to visit some similar institutions in England or in America.

"Have you such things in England and

America?"

"Yes, certainly. They are not called Palaces of the Pioneers, but we have Technical Schools, and Kindergartens, and Clubs for Children and Young People."

(The Palace of the Pioneers partakes of the nature of all these institutions, and has a really excellent Marionette-show in a special little theatre, into the bargain.)

"If you visited some of these places in other countries, you could compare them with your own. It would be very interesting."

"No," says the Comrade, employing the simple form of flat contradiction favoured by so many of the Comrades. "No, it would not be interesting. We do not wish to see how things are done in capitalist countries. When the foundation is wrong, the building cannot be right. We know that our way is better."

I should like to tell her the story of the two Army chaplains, of whom the Church of England padre said to his Roman Catholic colleague: "After all, you and I are both serving the same God," and met with the reply. "Yes, indeed. You in your way, and I in His."

[326]

I VISIT THE SOVIETS

But if I did tell her, she wouldn't think it funny.
Nor would she see its appᵤcation to the official
attitude of the U.S.S.R.

One can only congratulate the Government on
the thoroughness with which it has seen to it that
everyone coming into contact with foreign visitors
upholds the theory that Soviet Russia has attained
to earthly perfection within the last twenty years
and has no longer anything to learn.

I wish one could talk to the old people, or the
people living in remote villages, or the few remaining White Russians who still stay on and contrive
somehow to live.

Stories filter through, from time to time. . . .
Of people who try to get away and can't—of
people who live hunted lives, in cellars—of people
who are serving long terms of forced labour, as
prisoners. . . .

Nobody really knows the truth.

It is evident that enormous progress is being
made all over the country in civilization, and that
the coming generation is to have a fair chance of
acquiring health, and education, and a limited
amount of culture. (Limited, because everything
is forbidden that is not directly in sympathy with

[327]

Communist ideals, and because no society from
which individualism is excluded can ever hope to
produce creative artists.)

Perhaps it is inevitable that a country which has
fought its way from centuries of tyranny and
ignorance through bloody civil war, into the throes
of a colossal re-birth, should meet criticism with
this blind, aggressive self-assertion.

All the same, it is very far from prejudicing one
in favour of the Soviet system, to find so many of
its exponents without humour, without manners
and without imagination.

(2)

I am leaving Russia.

I sail from Odessa for Istanbul tonight.

I have still not spoken my mind.

In defiance of repeated instructions from Intourist—and also from many of my fellow-
travellers—to the effect that "tips are neither expected nor required in the Soviet Union"—I have
tipped several of the hotel servants, and they have
accepted my offerings without the slightest demur.

I have said goodbye to Intourist, and they to

me, without very much *abandon* on either side.

I have packed.

I have spent hours and hours debating within myself the best means of taking out of Russia a thirty-thousand-word manuscript containing the impressions of the new Mrs. Trollope on her travels. Sometimes I think that the general atmosphere of intrigue and mystery, so characteristic of the country, has quite gone to my head, and that there is in reality no reason at all why I shouldn't pack the manuscript in the ordinary way, amongst sponge-bags and pyjamas. At other times—mostly in the middle of the night, when judgments always tend to become melodramatic—I see the Customs officials seizing the manuscript, and the police seizing me, and each of us being taken away in a different direction. And I wonder how I shall be able to explain the position to my American publishers.

I have asked advice twice—which is a grave mistake because each adviser says something quite different. Both, however, are agreed that the Customs officials are a great deal more interested in books, papers, manuscripts and films than in any other form of contraband. This interest is manifested not only when one enters the country but, even more actively, when one leaves it.

Finally, I am decided by the frightful story of an American journalist in the Odessa hotel who tells me that he once wrote half a novel whilst he was in Russia, and put it in his suitcase to take to America, only to have to part with it at the Customs.

"They said they'd have to look through it," he disconsolately remarks. "That was eighteen months ago, and I guess they're still looking."

"Was it about Russia?"

"Nope. It was about night life in New York."

"Did you tell them that?"

"Yeah, sure I did. But they couldn't any of them read English, so they took it away to find someone who could."

I think of my own manuscript, entirely written in pencil, and feel that it may well take a very long while indeed before any persons are found who can read it. And when they do, they almost certainly won't like it.

"If you've written anything at all that you want to take home with you," says the American journalist significantly, "just carry it under your coat or somewhere. You'll find it saves a very great deal of time.

I think he is right.

He is less right when he adds:

"It's only for a few minutes, after all."

In my experience of Russia, nothing is ever done there in the space of a few minutes.

With an agreeable feeling that I am being like someone in a novel about international gangs, I draw the curtains and lock the door of my bedroom and proceed to wedge the manuscript against my spine, under my elastic belt.

It is agony.

I shall never endure it for five minutes, let alone five hours.

I remove the hard cover of the manuscript, find quite another part of my spine, and try again.

Bad, but endurable.

If I put on my loose coat now, I shall be much too hot, but I defy anybody to notice anything abnormal in my back view.

Besides, I shall face them all the time, and look them straight in the eyes with that directness of gaze which is well known to be the outward sign of utter rectitude of spirit.

The least agreeable of the guides has been given

the task of seeing off the departing tourists. There are only six of us: two Swedish astronomers, who came to see the eclipse of the sun, an elderly English couple, a young American College boy and myself.

We drive down to the docks: I see the last of the beautiful crescent of houses above the sea-front, the last of the two-hundred steps down to the Black Sea, the last of Karl Marx preening himself on the pedestal originally occupied by the probably better-looking statue of the Empress Catherine, the last of the town that I have liked best of all those I have visited in the U.S.S.R.

I have no regrets.

If I had any, I shouldn't be in a position to indulge in them, partly because I am preoccupied by the displeasing thought that, if I get much hotter, most of my manuscript will probably become blurred and undecipherable, and partly because I feel ill.

The fate that overtook the unhappy Miss Bolton has, even at the eleventh hour, also overtaken me.

Either the black bread, the salad—grown in a drain?—or the drinking-water, has chosen this inconvenient moment for taking its toll of me.

If I faint—and I feel as though, between the heat, my coat, and my indisposition I certainly shall—someone will have the brilliant idea of loosening my clothes, and the manuscript will fall out, and I shall come to under a strong police guard. . . .

I do not faint.

Instead, I get out of the car with everybody else, and we all go into a shed on the docks and the inevitable wait begins, and goes on, and goes on, and goes on.

A great number of rather *dégommés*-looking Comrades are scattered about the long shed, all engaged in their usual occupation of waiting. Their luggage includes bedding, little hand-carts, bundles of wraps—one of which startles me by suddenly turning out to be an old woman—bags, boxes and the customary mysterious portfolios.

Some of the Comrades eat dried fish.

Some of them sleep.

Almost all of them cough and spit.

"I wonder what we're waiting for," says the elderly Englishwoman.

She can't have been very long in Russia.

But the guide—as usual—has her answer.

"They are not yet ready," she says.

"The Customs officers?"

"They are busy."

As there are none of them in sight, the guide can't possibly know if they are busy or not. She just says it automatically. I admire the spirit of the elderly Englishwoman, who replies at once that they ought to be busy over our luggage, not over anything else.

The guide, for once, has nothing to say, and we all continue to await the pleasure of the Customs officials.

(By this time most of my pencilled records *must* have come off on my back.)

A little baby, swaddled to the eyebrows in shawls, screams and howls from behind its mufflings—as well it may. Nobody unwraps it, or takes much notice.

Nobody seems to be taking much notice of anything. We are all sunk in fatalistic apathy.

It is an atmosphere that seems very characteristic of a Russian gathering.

Even when the officials at last crawl in, one at a time from an inner office, nobody is in the least excited.

One or two of the people nearest the counter heave their luggage onto it and then turn aside in a dejected way, as though knowing that nothing is really going to happen yet, and ashamed of their own misguided impetuosity.

Only the elderly English couple, stalwart and determined, march up with their solid, respectable-looking suitcases and take up their stand in front of the counter. The guards at Waterloo probably looked like that, only with better effect, for the French are more impressionable than the Soviet Comrades by a very long way.

The College boy is consulting the guide about his films and his photographs. He has been consulting everybody about them, throughout the last two days. His predicament is very far from being peculiar to himself.

He has been in Russia four weeks and has taken a great many snapshots. Belatedly, he has discovered that no undeveloped films will be allowed to leave the country. Very well—he will have them developed and printed in Moscow. He does, and is asked to pay a sum in roubles that would handsomely buy up films, photographs, camera and all,

[335]

twice over. We have all heard of this outrage, and we have all assured him, with varying degrees of sympathy, that the same thing has happened to other tourists in the U.S.S.R. before now.

He seems unable to believe it.

I watch him, walking agitatedly to and fro, until a new wave of nausea comes over me and I clutch the sides of my bench and pass into a brief, unpleasant coma.

When I emerge, wet through and with the manuscript surely in worse case than ever, the College boy and his films are being dealt with by the officials.

Strip after strip of negatives is being unrolled, held up to the light and scrutinized. The inspection requires the full attention of all the Customs officials—not one is left to attend to anybody else.

The Comrades, seeming neither surprised nor resentful, continue to cough, spit, sleep or eat fish. The crying baby, still muffled, is being carried up and down by a young man with a beard, who holds a book in one hand and reads as he walks.

(Culture.)

The tourists mutter a little amongst themselves at the new delay, but are, I think, supported by the hope of some dramatic discovery, such as that the films include a snapshot of the interior of the Kremlin—(where nobody, except officials, is now allowed to set foot)—or a complete set of naval and military plans of the utmost importance.

Nothing of the kind transpires.

However, the last roll of all, which the American youth has not had the sense to slip into his pocket, has not been developed.

It is, says the young man, nothing. Just some pictures of the scenery in the Crimea.

Officials of any other nation might be expected to take one of two courses: either to accept this statement and pass the films or to reject it and confiscate them.

In Russia, the situation apparently calls for the formation of a kind of minor parliament.

The original officials send for more and higher officials, who come out of the main office one by one, mostly in shirt-sleeves, and gather solemnly round the little red cylinder lying on the counter.

The Intourist guide hovers about, talking a great deal and looking anxious.

"If you like, they will keep and have develop and send after you."

"That'll be very expensive, won't it?"

The guide shrugs her shoulders. We all know that it will be very expensive—and very uncertain into the bargain.

"Better let them go," advises the English-woman.

Her husband supports her, though he adds sternly that the *principle* of the thing is all wrong from start to finish.

The College boy, muttering that it's disgraceful, decides to let the films go. Twelve views of the Crimean scenery are lost for ever to the United States of America.

Nobody else's luggage yields anything sensational.

Mine is the last to be examined, owing to the qualms of sickness which keep on breaking over me and preventing me from moving.

Perhaps I am, after all, starting one of the illnesses against which I was solemnly inoculated before leaving England. I supposed inoculations wear off, after a time?

If it's smallpox, they won't let me leave the country.

Say nothing about it.

I VISIT THE SOVIETS

I would rather die at sea than in Russia.

"What is this?"

"A book."

"It is a book you got in Russia?"

Obviously, it is a book I got in Russia. It is a large album, with Russian text, containing some beautiful reproductions of the pictures in the gallery of Western Art at Moscow.

As it is large and heavy I have packed it in the bottom of my suitcase, and from thence it is extracted—with a bad effect on all the layers of things above it.

The conscientious Customs officials look through every single page of it. I do not know what they expect to find hidden between them. Perhaps they just like pictures.

My other books get off lightly—so do my clothes. My letter-case is turned inside out, my very small diary severely scrutinized, upside-down.

I am asked to open my hand-bag.

What shall I do if they suggest searching me?

They do not.

They repack my suitcases, quite obligingly, and shut them up again—the heavy Russian album is now on the top of my clothes instead of underneath them—and I have passed the Customs.

"Can I go through to the boat now?"

"You must wait a little," says the guide kindly. "You are tired, yes?"

I am, in my own opinion, at the point of death—but I do not say so.

"It's rather hot in here."

"There are many people."

The Comrades certainly do look numerous as they crowd round the long, dirty wooden counter on which their belongings are now being opened and examined.

The guide keeps on looking at me—no doubt I am pale green by now—and I feel I ought to distract her attention.

Would this be a good opportunity for speaking my mind, for the first and last time, in the Soviet Republic?

It must be now or never.

Quite suddenly, a crisis supervenes between the Customs officials and a middle-aged and rather battered-looking Comrade. He shouts, and they shout; he tries to get out at the far door that leads to where the boat is lying, and is prevented.

"What is the matter?"

"His passport is not in order. He cannot leave."

"Poor man!"

"He is upset because his family, they will have to go."

"Without him?"

"He cannot go. His passport is not in order."

"But they'll stay behind with him, won't they?"

"No, they will have to go. It is all arranged."

How very dreadful this is. . . . The unfortunate Comrade with the defective passport is now in tears on our side of the counter and his family on the other—two women, a little boy, a baby and the grandmother whom I mistook for a bundle.

They say goodbye, in a very spectacular way, across the counter, although I think there is really no reason why they should not all be on the same side.

"When will he be able to join them?"

"I cannot say."

"I think it would be far better if they all waited together, till his papers have been put in order."

"No," says the guide. "They cannot. They have given up their room. There is nowhere for them to be, now, except the ship."

And I realize that what she says is quite true.

I VISIT THE SOVIETS

The Swedish astronomers look disturbed, and say "Poor things!" and the College boy gives it as his considered opinion that Russia is *not* a free country, no sir, it is *not*.

The unfortunate family are saying goodbye again, and the baby is being handed to and fro across the counter repeatedly. It makes me, if possible, feel dizzier than before and I can watch them no longer.

The far door has been opened, I pass out— manuscript and all—along the dock and up the gangway and onto the waiting boat.

I am off the soil of Soviet Russia.

In the very next berth to ours lies the *Jan Rudzutak* in which I sailed from London Docks to Leningrad, months and months ago.

What a voyage that was, with Mrs. Pansy Baker and her Flea, the Canadian engineer, Miss Blake and Miss Bolton and all the rest of it!

Time and the Hour, I think sententiously, ride through the roughest day. And on the whole, I *have* found it a fairly rough day—though nothing, I must always remember, to what Mrs. Trollope, with her children, her pincushions and her bazaar, must have found *her* day.

I VISIT THE SOVIETS

This one ends on a note of unforeseen brightness, too.

The Comrade whom I left in such trouble amongst the officials is, at the eleventh hour, after all allowed to sail. He is hustled up the gangway and into the steerage and all his family receive him with cries and screams, and the baby is again bandied about from hand to hand.

"But how did he get through, if his passport wasn't in order?"

"Definitely, by bribery," says the English traveller.

He brings forward no particular evidence to support this statement, and I shall never know whether it is really true or not.

But I think that most probably it is.

So I go down to my dirty little cabin, and retrieve my manuscript and find it less damaged than I expected, and ask a steward if I can have a little brandy to restore me—but none comes—and have every intention of going on deck again to see the very last of Soviet Russia, but find, after all, that I can't stir, and must remain ignominiously prone until I feel better.

The ship has begun to move. The journey away

[343]

from Russia has started.

In a few minutes I think I shall be asleep, although a Russian loud-speaker is blaring jazz somewhere on deck, and a group of Comrades, apparently exactly outside the port-hole, is discussing the Government's new suggestion of making abortion illegal—just as it is in Capitalist countries.

I wish I *had* spoken my mind, just once, in the U.S.S.R. Even though I know that nobody would have paid any attention to it, and even though it occurs to me to wonder whether I am absolutely certain of what my mind really is, concerning the new Russia.

THE END